THE PREMIERS JOEY AND FRANK

"A voyeuristic and tantalizing trip through the workings of the government by a man who was there." — THE PILOT

"Rowe's stories paint not only an interesting picture of Rowe's own life, but the lives of the two men in which the book is named, and in the process, their greed, power and lust." — THE MUSE

"*The Premiers Joey and Frank* is crack for political junkies and will be a welcome gift for even the marginally interested observer of the political scene." — THE TELEGRAM

ROSIE O'DELL

"*Rosie O'Dell* is one of those books with such brilliant writing as to lull you into forgetting you're actually reading." — THE PILOT

"Yes, it's Bill Rowe—back this time with his third novel, which I think is by far his best. Probably one of the better novels to come out in the past few years—depending on your own tastes, of course." — THE NORTHEAST AVALON TIMES

"[A] deeply emotional page-turner by one of the country's finest writers." — MEGAN MURPHY, INDIGO

"This is a terrific story that hinges on a woman who is like quick-silver, running through all the cracks." — THE GLOBE AND MAIL

"It's well-written (Rowe is an experienced and accomplished writer), the characters are excellently drawn and much of the writing is just plain funny." — THE PEI GUARDIAN

DANNY WILLIAMS, PLEASE COME BACK

"With a mind—and a pen—as sharp as a paper cut, the elegant, affable Rowe remains Newfoundland's literary agent provocateur, provoking, teasing, sometimes coddling his subjects, but all the time digging towards truths that cause discomfort for the province's Who's Who and everyman alike." — THE BUSINESS POST

DANNY WILLIAMS: THE WAR WITH OTTAWA

"Interesting book about a successful Canadian politician . . ."
— THE GLOBE AND MAIL

"[Danny Williams] is captivating. [Bill Rowe] spares no punches."
— THE COMPASS

"The most interesting political book to be released in Canada in some time . . ." — THE BUSINESS POST

"Rowe's Ottawa chronicle [is] absorbing, humorous."
— THE TELEGRAM

"I quickly realized that this was not going to be a dry political memoir. To the contrary, not only is the book interesting and revealing of this contentious time, it is very funny in places."
— THE CHRONICLE HERALD

"An exciting read." — THE NEWFOUNDLAND QUARTERLY

"[One of] three of this year's most controversial and talked about political books." — THE HOUSE, CBC RADIO

"Rowe has a more humanistic side to politics. It is as if a citizen managed to be a fly on the wall while Danny Williams fought."
— CURRENT MAGAZINE

"An eye-opening, often hilariously funny, account of life among Ottawa power brokers and civil servants."
— CANADIAN LAWYER MAGAZINE

"Bill Rowe has a lot to say. There are dozens of interesting stories told, and comments passed on . . ."
— THE NORTHEAST AVALON TIMES

"A fascinating and frequently funny read." — DOWNHOME

"Written with the knowledge and insight that only an insider could possess, this book (sub-titled 'The Inside Story of a Hired Gun') is a timely reminder of the duplicity of far too many of our elected leaders—no matter what their political stripe."
— ATLANTIC BOOKS TODAY

"The writer's good English style—rare today—his knowledge of all kinds of personalities in the political world and his misadventures in getting a basic office set up (which took six of the eight months he was there) all make for amusing and exciting reading."
— THE PEI GUARDIAN

The Monster
of Twenty Mile Pond

BY BILL ROWE

The Monster
of Twenty Mile Pond

Bill Rowe

FLANKER PRESS LIMITED

ST. JOHN'S

Library and Archives Canada Cataloguing in Publication

Rowe, William N. (William Neil), 1942-, author
    The monster of Twenty Mile Pond / Bill Rowe.

Issued in print and electronic formats.
ISBN 978-1-77117-369-8 (pbk.).--ISBN 978-1-77117-370-4 (epub).--
ISBN 978-1-77117-371-1 (kindle).--ISBN 978-1-77117-372-8 (pdf)

    I. Title.

PS8585.O8955M66 2014   C813'.54   C2014-903437-7
                                                C2014-903438-5

PRINTED IN CANADA

 This paper has been certified to meet the environmental and social standards of the Forest Stewardship Council® (FSC®) and comes from responsibly managed forests, and verified recycled sources.

Cover Design by Graham Blair   Edited by Susan Rendell

FLANKER PRESS LTD.
PO BOX 2522, STATION C
ST. JOHN'S, NL
CANADA

TELEPHONE: (709) 739-4477   FAX: (709) 739-4420   TOLL-FREE: 1-866-739-4420
WWW.FLANKERPRESS.COM

9 8 7 6 5 4 3 2 1

   Canada Council Conseil des Arts
                       for the Arts   du Canada

We acknowledge the financial support of the Government of Canada through the Canada Book Fund (CBF) and the Government of Newfoundland and Labrador, Department of Tourism, Culture and Recreation for our publishing activities. We acknowledge the support of the Canada Council for the Arts, which last year invested $157 million to bring the arts to Canadians throughout the country. *Nous remercions le Conseil des arts du Canada de son soutien. L'an dernier, le Conseil a investi 157 millions de dollars pour mettre de l'art dans la vie des Canadiennes et des Canadiens de tout le pays.*

The Monster
of Twenty Mile Pond

CHAPTER one

My intentions were good that golden summer afternoon. I was off to visit my beloved, as Ramona then was, to propose marriage. Driving away from my one-room flat, heading out of the city toward her family's splendid house overlooking the sea in the Cove, I rummaged about in my mind for the protocol I should employ to negotiate her sire's consent. I pictured her standing with her mother outside the closed door, both of them giggling at how cute and awkward her boyfriend and her daddy were being on the other side of it. She still called him Daddy. What did she do that for, at twenty-three? It had sounded charming when I'd first met her, but it had lately begun to get mildly on my nerves. What, by the way, if Daddy said no?

But I heard him now in my mind's ear interrupting my opening gambit: "I thought you'd never ask," he muttered low, so as not to be heard on the other side of the door. "The answer is yes. What were you waiting for? Yes. Yes. Yes." I was intuiting, perhaps with some slight exaggeration, that Daddy wouldn't be that much of a challenge. He plainly loved his daughter dearly, if "Ask and you shall receive" constituted fatherly love, but he did not give the impression of wanting to detain her as a resident of his home any longer than strictly necessary.

It was the same with Mommy. Yes, she called her Mommy still. Last month when I complimented Mommy again on the house and the superb view, she said, "Don't be intimidated by this house, Bill. I'm sure Ramona could get used to living in something small and unpretentious for a little while."

A couple of weeks ago, I'd heard Daddy whisper ferociously to Mommy in the kitchen, "What is it with her? She's so bloody contrary and pigheaded about every damn thing."

To which Mommy sighed, "I know, I know. But this too shall pass. Soon—be patient—it's coming soon, soon . . ."

I mentioned that parental exchange, which had sounded like they were desperate for a bailout, to my wise older sister, Maggie, and asked her what I was missing, because I didn't find my divine Ramona that way at all.

Maggie put her arm around my neck and looked sideways into my face with a droll smile. "No, of course you don't, my Billy boy," she said, "because now you two only meet to kiss and cuddle, if that's the right word. But just wait till you're walled in with her every breakfast, dinner, and bedtime, and she unearths a few irksome habits of yours—that might bring it out in her."

Motoring along Portugal Cove Road, I reached Windsor Lake,

still called Twenty Mile Pond by old-timers who liked to bring to mind the distance around its shores. I was always partial to that ancient, down-to-earth name myself, and wished it had never been changed.

There was a northwest wind crossing the water and the sun was low in the sky; objects stood out starkly and looked unnaturally close.

Maybe that was why the crows were squawking out a raucous din louder and in greater numbers than I'd ever heard before. My eyes were drawn to a wide-winged osprey soaring high above the lake. That magnificent raptor and its mate, called seahawks by some, were a common sight that summer, and the constant talk of people was the joy of catching sight of one abruptly diving from a lofty height to the water far below, and seizing a trout in its talons.

Preoccupied by wavering thoughts in my head, I glanced under the sun at the long, gilded stream of shimmering waves, and the two or three seagulls gliding above them. A striking image all at once filled my vision. It was the osprey. The great bird was just above the waves, and struggling to hover there, talons spread, as if it had brought its dive to a hasty, unforeseen halt. Then, in a merest instant, through the dazzle of light, I glimpsed a snakelike limb whip out of the water near the osprey, seize a seagull from midair, and vanish with it beneath a splash of spume and foam.

I jerked the car across the road into a space by the shore and stopped. The osprey was already climbing fast, propelled by the thrusts of its mighty five-foot wings. I swept my eyes over the lake for many minutes, but nothing appeared on its surface again; I could see only the glittering crests of waves. At last, I moved my car onto the road, but instead of continuing toward the house overlooking the sea, I turned around and drove back to my little room in the city, the plans in my head altered utterly.

"But why?" Ramona beseeched me. "Why are you doing this? We're so perfect together." I had no answer for her, especially since I well realized that I was giving up the woman who physically excited me more than anyone else I'd ever met. What was I to say to her? That I was doing it because I'd seen or, more likely, hallucinated, a tentacle emerging from Twenty Mile Pond and snatching, and dragging under, a pitiable gull that looked a lot like me?

I said nothing. But perhaps I should have answered her question. She may have been more content if she'd understood that the man who was breaking up with her was a raving lunatic. As it happened, though, she was the one who turned out to be, in the practical sense, if not the clinical, the raving lunatic.

She married one of my fellow lawyers a couple of years after, and their relationship steadily degenerated. Her healthy appreciation of wine when I'd known her became a serious drinking problem. Her husband found out from a colleague that she'd been unfaithful to him in a Montreal hotel, after a binge in the bar. He suspected she'd also developed a codeine habit.

None of these facets of her character were clearly evident when I knew her, but in retrospect I was not amazed that they'd emerged. When her husband separated from her, she used every force and power at her command—the female judge called it "sheer spite and vindictiveness"—to try to deprive him of shared custody of their two kids, or even of regular access to them. At one point she went public to allege that the "lawyers' union" had ganged up on her with the judges to support one of their own, and were criminally conspiring against her.

I ran into the ex-hubby years later at the Ship Inn, and he told me ruefully over a beer that I owed him big time.

"What for?" I asked.

With a drawn-out shake of his head and a woebegone grin, he replied, "For not marrying her when you had the chance."

Never again, after that life-changing day, did I see anything like my vision of the glorious seahawk and the doomed seagull. And I never heard tell of anything lurking beneath the waves of Twenty Mile Pond that could have produced that tentacle. Not until now, twenty-two years later.

CHAPTER two

Our seventeen-year-old niece, Esme, was as wilful as she was lovely, my wife and I both agreed, and as unruly as she was bright. She was starting to cause us more woe than our own two kids combined. What had once been just exasperating had become worrisome, especially since her cousin, our own, slightly younger daughter, Molly, was also her loyal and constant companion.

I was inclined to be lenient, even indulgent, with Esme. After the tragedy that had befallen her five years before, I found her behaviour to be—no, not reasonable, but understandable, and my relentless awareness of what she'd been through gave me the desire and strength to bear with her.

That was probably why I considered her first infractions fairly minor. When she was fourteen, for example, she'd been caught smoking with an older girl in the school washroom. She reported to me afterwards, with a contrite smile, that the principal had kicked her out of school for three days. It should only have been for two days, she said, but when he demanded why she had broken the rule of absolutely no smoking by anyone in the school, she'd replied, "I'm not allowed to sneak one in the staff room and blow the smoke out the window like some teachers do." Bingo, an extra day off for being so smart-alecky.

I told her I was more concerned with her smoking in the first place than with her doing it in school. She replied that I was not to worry; she was not asinine enough to start smoking, and the whole thing had been an egregious—her word—mistake on her part that would not recur. When the principal called me, knowing from her mother, my sister, Maggie, that I was helping with Esme's parenting, he said that, normally, in these circumstances, she could have been expelled.

"For smoking?" I responded in surprise.

"They weren't smoking tobacco," he replied. "The teacher who caught them smelled marijuana, but the girls managed to flush the joint down the toilet." So the principal used the lack of physical evidence and her good grades, plus her traumatic history, to tone down the punishment. Besides, our daughter Molly had told her teacher that Esme had only been experimenting on herself about the effects of cannabis because she'd read online that the drug could have a calming influence on the kind of muscle spasms that afflicted her mother.

"I have my reservations about Esme's noble experiment, myself," the principal went on, "not having just fallen off the turnip truck, but I gave her the benefit of the doubt this one time, anyway." Yes, we both agreed, normally Esme was a wonderful young lady.

Then, when Esme was fifteen, her mother, Maggie, called me at midnight on a Friday. "Two policemen just brought my daughter home," Maggie laboured to say, "and deposited her on the doorstep, drunk. If she passes out and throws up, I mightn't be able to help her." I released my wife's amorous hold on me with apologies and regret, and pecked her pursed lips. She patted my shoulder as if she was consoling the loser in a squash tournament, and I hauled on a sweatsuit to drive over to Maggie's.

Esme was sprawled on the sofa. Seeing me, she lurched up straight and pulled at her skirt, which had ridden well up over her knees; the black tights had a run in one leg which extended to the ankle. Her lipstick was smeared, and her hair, as our father used to describe boisterous young Maggie's own, was like a birch broom in the fits. Despite her disarray, my wife's comment of a few weeks ago was still apt: "She's an alarmingly gorgeous creature." Two unopened bottles of beer were on the coffee table in front of her. The police had found them in her handbag.

In a low voice and thick words, she protested to me against the overreaction of the police in raiding the party. The complaints they'd received of loud noise, underage drinking, and fights were unwarranted. "And on top of that, Uncle Bill," she slurred earnestly, "the cops violated everyone's privacy by taking down our names. This police brutality will go down in the history of North America"—she paused for effect but couldn't resist a grin—"as the Friday Night Massacre."

"Not funny," said Maggie.

"Wasn't this the same party," I asked, "that Molly was at? She was home by ten o'clock."

"Yesh, and she toally"—I think she was trying to say "totally"—"begged me to leave with her when the beer started to arrive, but"—Esme abruptly gained her feet and weaved down the hall, her mouth scrunched tight and her cheeks ballooning. Maggie sighed and started wheeling after her. I placed my hand on her shoulder and said I'd go.

When I entered the bathroom, Esme was on her knees holding on to the sides of the porcelain bowl for dear life and vomiting violently into it. In between paroxysms, her face threatened to sag down into the mess, and I gently held her head back while I flushed. At the sight of her anguished, beautiful young face, my tears began to flow. She seemed to be in such emotional pain.

My mind flashed back to when she was a little girl of eight, a few years before the accident, when she'd stood solidly in front of me and said, "Uncle Bill, Dad says that my name has to go back thousands of years. He says there was a very old language that a lot of languages these days came from—English, Spanish, Russian, and lots of others—languages all the way from Portugal to India and North and South America. He says my name looks like it comes from an old word that meant 'I am.' It's still the same sound, almost, in English and other languages now, years and years later. Esme, I am, is me—get it? Cool, huh?"

"Very cool," I'd said. "To have stayed the same so long means those sounds must have been something people everywhere wanted to keep forever."

When she stopped being sick in the bathroom, I left her there to wash her face and went out to sit with my sister. She stayed silent, looking at the floor. "No big deal, Maggie," I said. "Growing pains."

"You think?"

"Remember that time," I said, "—what were you, sixteen?—when you sneaked out your bedroom window two o'clock in the morning, climbed down from the garage roof to meet your friend, and both of you hightailed it off to rendezvous with your boyfriends in Bannerman Park? Do I recall correctly that there was Portuguese brandy involved that you got from some sailors off the White Fleet, and that Dad grounded you for a month and—"

"Okay, okay," said Maggie, raising her left hand a little, the hand she could move, from the armrest of her wheelchair. "You've got a good memory, Billy boy. But look how well I turned out." She snorted out a laugh.

Esme crept back into the room. "I don't blame you for laughing," she murmured. "Because I've been really stupid. I'm so sorry, Mom and Uncle Bill. I only meant to have a bit of fun. It won't happen—"

"I wasn't laughing at you, Esme," said Maggie. "There was nothing funny about what you did tonight. And it was beyond really stupid. More like really moronic. And, sweetheart, I know it won't happen again, because, just as we love you, we know you love us."

Esme closed her eyes and nodded at her mother.

"Can I help you into bed, Maggie?" I asked.

"No, I will," said Esme. "I'll get the medicine." Maggie's

medication, I knew, was to prevent the painful muscle spasms that would otherwise keep her awake most of the night.

Esme still looked shaky, so I sat in the living room and waited until Maggie's preparations for bed were completed. It must have taken a half-hour or more, a lot of it spent in the bathroom.

I'd asked Maggie a few times if she should have extra home care for a couple of hours at night before bed, but she always declined. "It's already costing an arm and a leg, no pun intended, for the six hours I have now. We'll cut that back soon, too." And Esme would chime in that she could do the nighttime care because she was usually home from her part-time job before her mother went to bed. No, I could never deny that, usually, Esme was a great girl.

CHAPTER three

A few months after the drunken episode, Esme and two other female teenaged scofflaws were charged with shoplifting at one of the bargain stores. They were accused of stealing hiking socks, of all things. My daughter Molly had been with them, but in another aisle altogether when they got caught, and was not implicated. Somehow Esme always managed to keep Molly out of the trouble she got into herself.

I may be a lawyer, but I'm a civil lawyer with very little idea of any criminal law procedures, let alone those under the Youth Criminal Justice Act, so I put a smart young associate with the firm on her case. His name was Brian Keeping and he came back from his meeting with Esme like someone in love. "She's a really funny girl," he said, grinning like a chimpanzee.

"What do you mean by funny, precisely?" I asked. "Funny ha ha, or funny yikes?"

"Oh, definitely funny ha ha. She's got a great sense of humour. She says our defence should be that the aisles at the store are made deliberately narrow, so that all the merchandise is close as you pass it, and that no normal mortal could resist grabbing something and shoving it under their jacket. We have to convince the judge, she says, that the store is to blame for luring and entrapping their customers into shoplifting." Brian laughed, utterly charmed.

I shared none of his appreciation of my niece's precocious judicial brilliance. "Just get her out of this," I muttered. And lo, Brian, by some intervention procedure, or diversion program, or extrajudicial whatnot, all invented by the caring professions, managed to do just that.

Molly told me that Esme had really needed those socks—that she'd developed a horrendous blister on the side of her little toe on their last hike—but she didn't have the money to pay for them.

"Didn't have the money to pay for a pair of socks? What's she doing with the money she makes at the fast-food place?"

"Dad, Esme will kill me if she hears I told you this. Her mother's credit card is up on bust, but she made Esme swear she wouldn't let you know. Aunt Maggie is doing everything to cut down on expenses, but stuff costs so much. . . . Every single cent Esme makes goes to her mother. Dad, the only time she's a little bit happy is when she's on a long hike in the woods."

I wished to myself that Maggie would let me know of these needs before her daughter ended up down in the penitentiary. But I well realized how keenly she felt that she was a burden on my family, and it made her very reticent about her financial problems.

I arranged to funnel more money to her with a soft suggestion that she let me know if Esme needed anything else to outfit her for her hiking or any other positive pastime.

The second-last serious incident, the one before the current catastrophe, involved a wild animal. Esme and Molly and some of their friends were walking on one of the footpaths in the rich trail system of St. John's. Esme was carrying her hiking pole with her. We all knew, because she told us, that her pole was not to assist her in walking, but served solely as protection. I'm sure she got that idea from me. A few months earlier, after a walk on Signal Hill, I'd complained to my wife in front of the girls that some dog owners allowed their big, poop-bloated mutts to run around off their leashes and leave their business wherever and whenever on the trails, which was all bad enough, *but*, if one of those pit bulls or huge mastiffs with their massive jaws took it into its head to attack me or anyone else near me, it would be their last act. I was getting a nice, handy, steel-tipped hiking pole. I never did, but a while later, there was Esme, lifting and wielding her pole with a fencer's dexterity to display her skill and its sharp metal point. Being all too familiar with her history, I couldn't fault her for being hyper-cautious in the face of animals that could injure or kill.

The girls weren't familiar with the trail they were walking on that day; they tried to choose a different one each time. They were surprised when a grey fox bounded out of the underbrush toward them. But then the animal stopped and swerved toward two women walking along ahead of them with young children.

Molly said afterwards that the fox really looked to them like it was about to attack the kids, the way it quickly slunk along, low to the ground, ears back, teeth clearly showing. The parents of the children insisted to the police, however, that it was merely being friendly, as it always was. Whatever the case, Esme lunged toward the fox and took a ferocious swing at it with her pole. She missed it by inches—deliberately, she would contend afterwards—and the fox snarled and made guttural sounds as it stood its ground, crouching. Esme swung at it again, this time grazing the fox's back with the point of her pole.

The women and kids erupted in shrieks as the fox snarled and then backed away yelping before it turned and scurried into the underbrush. The girls gathered from the screams and wailing that the women and children were familiar with the fox and believed that it was only approaching them in the hope of food. One of the women called the police on her cellphone and the girls hung around until they arrived.

Esme told the police that, judging by the look of the fox and the way it had approached, she believed it to be rabid. The women yelled that that was utter nonsense: there was a whole family of foxes nearby that everyone knew about and which had become friendly with people. They would come within feet of hikers, who often tossed food to them. Everyone knew that foxes on the Avalon didn't have rabies. The police took names and addresses and the next day they laid charges against Esme under the animal cruelty laws for wilful abuse of a protected animal.

I put our young lawyer, Brian Keeping, on this case, too, and he insisted to the police that one of foxes be trapped and tested for disease. Upon their refusal, he had to obtain a court order requiring wildlife officers to trap a fox and test it. The prosecution was arguing that everyone familiar with the locale knew the foxes had been there for months and were as tame and friendly as household pets. But, to everyone's shock, except Esme's, the tests showed that the fox in fact did carry the beginnings of rabies; the disease was in the stage known as the prodromal, usually associated in wild animals with unusual behaviour, including overfamiliarity and aggression toward humans. The whole family of foxes had to be trapped and destroyed.

The charges were dropped, and one of the women on the trail was quoted in the newspaper thanking the young lady for "perhaps" saving their kids from a rabid bite. She seemed rather dubious, though, that Esme could have known of the rabies from a glance at the fox, since the vet had said that even a trained wildlife expert would have had difficulty in distinguishing the fox's rabies symptoms from its conditioned sociability. I had a chat about all this with my niece and daughter.

I told Esme straight that she had been spared criminal conviction by pure dumb luck. She went very quiet for a minute and closed her eyes. Then tears began to flow from under her eyelids, although she didn't cry. "I'm sorry, Uncle Bill," she said, "but I did know that the fox was sick. I just knew. I love animals a lot, but if I see a situation where an animal might hurt some innocent person, I'm going to act." She lowered her head almost down to her hands on her lap, and shook with silent sobs. Molly and I went over to her and put our arms around her, and I knew that all three of us were meditating on the devastating accident that had happened to her family when Esme was twelve years old.

CHAPTER four

Esme's father, Jack Browning, was an impressive, likeable man. He never advanced this information, but Maggie told me he was co-laterally related to the poet Robert Browning. His great-great-great-grandfather, like Robert Browning's grandfather, was part owner of a plantation worked by slaves in the West Indies, and his great-great-grandfather, like Robert Browning's father, became revolted by the slavery and left the Caribbean. The poet's father went back to England; Jack's ancestor went to Canada.

Maggie had met Jack in Ontario when she was studying social work on a scholarship at Queen's University. Jack was an engineer, ten years older than Maggie. He had an affiliation with the university and was married with two sons, three and four years old. He and Maggie discovered they both had a great affinity for English language and literature. They would have done graduate work in English at university and written poetry and novels, they told each other, had they not both subscribed to rule number one for any prospective writer: pay the darn rent. Hence, engineering and social work became their income earners. Jack fell hard for Maggie.

Maggie didn't encourage him beyond friendship, she always told me—heavens, he was a married family man—but he stayed in touch with her when she came back here. Then, out of the blue, without conferring with Maggie, she said, he separated, got a divorce, and moved to St. John's to pursue her. His ardour broke up the engagement between Maggie and her fiancé. She married him; six months later Esme was born.

Twelve years after that, Esme and her mother and father were driving from St. John's to Trinity on the Bonavista Peninsula. They were to join another family there, spend a couple of nights at a B & B, and explore the region. Molly had been due to go with them, but she had to cancel because of a bout of food poisoning. They had been planning to leave right after work on Friday, but the delay caused by Esme's futile attempt to persuade Molly out of her sickbed meant an hour's driving after dark. With the ever-present danger of a collision with a moose, especially as rutting season approached, nighttime driving was taboo.

They left early Saturday morning with Jack behind the wheel, Maggie in the front passenger seat, and Esme in the back seat. She had been silent and sad, she told me, still wishing that Molly had been well enough to go. Jack had the cruise control set at 109 kilometres an hour, acting on his theory that the RCMP never ticketed people for speeding if they were driving under 110.

Not far from the Come By Chance turnoff on the clear, dry Trans-Canada Highway, Jack was looking at Esme in the rearview mirror and asking what CD she'd like to hear, and Maggie was turning her head to smile at her daughter, when Esme saw, between them through the windshield, directly ahead, a big bull moose bounding out of the ditch onto the road. Seconds went by before she could speak. Just after she shouted "Dad, watch out!" their car struck the moose.

The huge animal with its long spindly legs was just the right height to slide up over the hood of the car and crash through the windshield. An unimaginable stench was Esme's immediate sensation. According to the police report, the moose's belly had been ripped open on impact with the front of the vehicle. The car rolled off the pavement and plowed along the shoulder and the shallow ditch for many metres before coming to a stop, still upright.

That position was an unfortunate fluke, the investigators said, because if the car had turned over a couple of times, the beast may well have been shaken loose. But the moose stayed attached to the car, with most of its torn belly inside enveloping Jack's head and face. A rear hoof had also come through the broken glass.

Esme could hear her father's horrible groans. Meanwhile, the rear hoof of the animal was kicking and thrashing, and Esme saw it strike her mother on the side of the head. Esme undid her seat belt and tried to help her father, but it was all she could do to keep her face away from the moose's flailing hoof. It struck her forearm, laying open the skin and breaking the bone.

She pushed open her door and got out, with the intention of

trying to pull her father from under the moose with one hand. The front part of the moose, from its forelegs to its huge head and antlers, projected past the side of the car, barring her way. As people picked their routes down the slight slope from the road, waving and shouting, one big moose eye stared at Esme, wide with terror. (Then it seemed to become sad, she told us later; the last thing she saw was the eye glazing over in death.) And the last thing she heard were her own screams: "Get Dad out, get Dad *out!*" and "Help Mom. He kicked Mom in the head."

But they couldn't get her dad out in time; when they got him out, he was dead. The ambulance attendants applied whatever techniques they could to her mom. Maggie was alive but unconscious, and her skull appeared to be fractured. Esme went into shock, and some anonymous person wrapped her up in a blanket to keep her warm and applied a tourniquet to her arm, which the ambulance attendants, when they arrived, credited with saving her life.

In hospital, lying in bed with her arm in a sling, Esme surprised us by musing softly on how ironic the police statement was, the part where they claimed that excessive speed may have contributed to the accident. In fact, their car had been the slowest one on the road, she murmured, with all the other vehicles passing it like it was going backwards. No, it wasn't caused by Dad driving too fast, she said; she herself had caused the accident. What happened was all her fault.

He wouldn't have been looking back at her in the first place, trying to cheer her up, if she hadn't been acting like a contrary child. And she had let seconds go by after seeing the moose before alerting her father. If she'd told him at once, with his reflexes—everyone knew how good Dad was in goal in the masters hockey league—he could have missed the moose completely. He would've had about thirty metres, nearly a hundred feet, to work with.

My wife, Jennifer, and I looked at each other. Esme had it all calculated out, the mathematics that proved her dreadful guilt.

"Esme," said Molly, "you aren't—"

"I am," Esme said, dry-eyed and gaunt-faced. "Dad said that my name shouts out 'I am.' But honest to God, I wish I wasn't. 'I am not' would be better."

I kissed her temple and we all stayed quiet for a while. Molly and I held her free hand. Then Esme murmured, "Dad's great-great-great-uncle Robert could have written a pretty good poem about this: 'The glorious fruit of illicit love leads relentless to death by moose guts—Oh, the grandeur and the splendour.'"

That night, Jennifer said to me, "My God, Bill, did you hear her? 'The fruit of illicit love leads to death by moose guts'? On top of all the blame? She's twelve years old, for heaven's sake. She's more than traumatized by this. She's . . . you—we—need to keep a close watch on this."

A few years before that, Jack and Maggie had started a construction business, and were doing pretty well. Jack managed the fieldwork and Maggie ran the office. Two months before the accident, their company had won a sizable road building contract. The job was a big challenge, but their smarts and work ethic were carrying them on their way to prosperity. After the accident, though, with Jack's key-man life insurance going to investors, with their house mortgaged to the hilt to cover their own investment, with the government's decision to pass the contract over to another company under the completion bond, my sister was broke and in debt.

She was also severely paralyzed. In a coma for two weeks, Maggie emerged into consciousness following operations to remove a large blood clot from her brain and to repair the damage to her skull. She had no use of her right side, arm or leg, and restricted use of her left side. After a number of months, her speech came back, just a little laboured, and her intelligence began to restore itself. But her physical condition, which included incapacitating headaches and muscle spasms, meant she would not be able to work for a long time, perhaps forever.

I did the best I could on her behalf by threatening lawsuits, backed by the full force of the law firm's reputation, and succeeded in salvaging a pathetic $100,000 for her out of the construction company's wreckage. Even with extremely frugal management, considering the costs of a decent wheelchair and other mobility equipment, plus proper nursing assistance at home, much of which would not be paid for by the government, the money could only last a year or so. Then Maggie and Esme would be on welfare.

I was going to have to tell my wife that I couldn't let this happen to my sister and my niece: she and I would be looking at a huge burden of care and expenses. We could expect no help from anywhere else. Jack's parents had sided from the beginning with his first wife, and every extra dollar they had they spent on her two boys, now at university, and on their other grandchildren. My mother had nothing to spare from my deceased father's meagre civil service pension. I thought I knew what to expect from Jennifer: she'd smile and shoulder the burden with me without complaint, but I wondered in unspoken anxiety how this would tax our excellent marriage.

CHAPTER *five*

I'd met Jennifer Ward in a courtroom just weeks after breaking up with Ramona on the day of my vision by Twenty Mile Pond. She was a new accountant and a minor witness in our opponent's case. She was there to back up the testimony given by the senior main witness. I was junior counsel, so my mentor put me up to cross-examining this junior witness to hone my non-existent skills.

During my questioning, I told her—kindly, I thought—that I was having some difficulty grasping whatever point it might be that she was struggling so hard to make. She smiled sweetly and said, "You may not understand my point, sir, but then exhaustive studies have shown that the IQ of the average chartered accountant is significantly higher than that of the average lawyer."

Everyone in the courtroom laughed, including the judge, and of course I joined in as a good sport, pretending I didn't mind one little bit having the tables turned on me and being made to look like a clown. But I stopped being kind to her, and gradually went aboard of her verbally to the point where, a couple of times, her client's lawyer objected that I was badgering the witness. After I was finished, the other lawyer asked the judge for a recess, with our consent, to explore a possible settlement. The judge retired to his chambers, and the matter was in fact settled within an hour right there in the courtroom.

During the discussion, Jennifer murmured to me, "By the way, Mr. McGill, you didn't have to get so mad at me. I said 'average lawyer.'" Then, while we were waiting for the judge to come back to adjourn the case *sine die*, she glanced at the other lawyer, and leaned toward me and said, "After the hosing you guys just gave our client, I'm going to be recommending to all our clients from now on that they retain your firm." She smiled at me. "I certainly don't want to go through that ever again."

My mentor at the firm didn't offer the high opinion of my performance that Jennifer had, but then, as she told me a couple of weeks later over dinner in a fancy restaurant, he hadn't been trying to sweet-talk me into asking him out.

We married within a couple of years, had our daughter Molly and son Matthew in quick succession, and were on our way to living happily ever after. We got on our feet financially and were planning major renovations to our lovely old house and annual family travel vacations—this year up the Nile for the four of us, next year the Mediterranean. All of which adventures were now jeopardized or completely off the table as a result of what had happened to Maggie and Esme.

I was in the process of telling Jennifer I was sorry that my sister's accident would set back many of our dreams, when she put her fingers on my lips. "Maggie and Esme are part of our own family from now on," she said, "and entitled to exactly the same attention and financial support in every way as ourselves. If necessary, I'll go back to full-time practice." That would more than double the twenty-hour week she was punching in now, trying to juggle home and profession.

"How on earth did I get someone as compassionate and understanding as you to marry me?"

"I never let that stand in my way," she replied. "You never would've proposed if you knew you'd have to struggle so hard to keep up."

While Maggie was in the hospital recuperating and then at the Miller Centre for therapy, Esme lived at our house. I was about to clear out my home office to provide her with her own bedroom, but she and Molly insisted on using the same room. "We'll just move in another single bed," Molly whispered to me when we were alone in the kitchen. "Esme won't be happy here if she has to turf you out of your den."

Already close, the two became inseparable. "Joined at the hip," is how schoolmates started to describe them, which progressed to "and at the shoulder, the neck, and the head, to boot."

When Maggie came out of the Miller Centre and was pronounced capable of living on her own with nursing assistance, she wouldn't hear of staying with us. Everyone needed their space, she said. Esme went back home, too, much to our regret. We loved having her with us. Apart from the times we could see her melancholia coming on and she went for long walks alone or with Molly, my niece and my daughter had been a constant source of bright amusing chatter, livening up the house.

Esme even treated our son, Matthew, nearly two years her junior, with a respect and consideration not always present from Molly alone. They went to many of his minor hockey games at Esme's suggestion, where their presence and enthusiasm, more than Jennifer's or my own, we knew, encouraged him to rise to all-star team status in the Atom and Pee Wee divisions.

Matthew teased both girls that the high school players all wanted to be his best friend as soon as they learned that those two "hotties" leaning over the boards were his cousin and his sister. It was almost too adorable for Jennifer and me to bear as we listened from the kitchen to the three of them earnestly discussing hockey strategy for Matthew in the TV room, while the show on the screen went ignored.

The financial situation did become more onerous than I expected because of Maggie's unforeseen expenses, which she would never tell me about. I had to extract the data from her as if I was pulling teeth. And of course Esme's occasional falling off the rails, once she moved back home, added to the load.

When I complained to Jennifer in private in order to dig out her true feelings, she only said, "The poor little girl. When you think of what she's been through . . . I think Esme is forever in pain. Not only for herself, but for Maggie. I heard her mention to Molly that she can't bear what her mother has to suffer every night, unable to sleep a wink because of constant muscle spasms. The medicine doesn't seem to be working very well. So, Esme's experiment with the pot makes sense. And the beer that time? I'd say she feels driven sometimes to try to self-medicate her distress, her agony, away."

"And the shoplifting and the impulsive attack on the fox? That fits in with her self-medication how, exactly?"

"Yeah, okay, touché." She came over to me. "You're starting to turn me on. I feel like I'm back on the witness stand facing the world's greatest cross-examiner again. Anyway, I just hope she doesn't fall in with the hard drug crowd as she thrashes her way through this."

Jennifer's words were like a cue in a stage play.

CHAPTER six

I was in Calgary when Molly called me on my cellphone. Early on, I'd told her—and Jennifer and Matthew and Esme and Maggie—to call me on my cell at any time, any place, about anything, and if it was an emergency, and I didn't answer on the first call, to call me twice in rapid succession and I would answer it immediately no matter what I was doing or who I was with. Usually I loved it when they now and again actually did the double call. It made me feel like the best husband, father, uncle, and brother going, even if their definition of an emergency was somewhat looser than mine.

Once I said to Molly, upon taking her rapid second call on the cell outside my office door while my client anxiously paced the floor inside, that perhaps her request for permission to buy tickets to a Tragically Hip concert scheduled six months down the road might not qualify as an emergency. To which she rejoined, "Dad, *what*? They're selling like hotcakes. Da-*ad*, this is what fathers are *for*."

I was about to start the meeting in Calgary with the leaders of a consortium who were going to develop a multi-billion dollar oil reserve on the Grand Banks of Newfoundland. They wanted to talk personally with us, the principals of the local St. John's law firm recommended by their main firm in Calgary. When the phone vibrated in my pocket, I ignored it and prayed that it wouldn't buzz again.

When it immediately throbbed a second time, feeling like a jackhammer against my kidney, I saw looks of irritation exchanged between the executives as I rose and said I had to take an emergency call. They'd made it clear that they always liked meetings to start right on time. The exasperation on my partners' faces said to me, "Now, McGill, don't you bugger this up." I left the boardroom and took the call outside in the hall.

"Dad," Molly said, "the police have arrested Esme. You need to talk to them."

"The police what? Molly, get hold of Brian Keeping. I can't talk right now, I'm in the middle of a big meeting. What have they arrested her for?"

"They're saying it was a drug deal gone bad."

"A what? A drug deal gone—oh, for the love of—what is this, Molly, a Hollywood gangster movie? Where is she? I'll call Brian myself and ask him to handle it. He and Esme should be getting used to each other by now."

"Dad, you'd better come back. The police say they're going to charge her with murder—second-degree murder, they said."

"Murd—what? Good Lord. What about you? Were you involved, too?"

"Not in the actual murder itself. But I was in the car waiting for her. The police said they're still trying to figure out what to do with me."

"My God. Don't say anything to the police, sweetheart—you or her. Tell them you're waiting till your lawyer gets there. Where are you now?"

"I think Esme already told them what happened. I heard them say it was the most ridiculous story they ever heard. They were even laughing, Dad, and here's this guy lying on the ground dead."

"Molly, where are you?"

"We're in police cars out by Windsor Lake. But they're taking us in to the police station."

"I'll tell Brian to meet you there. Let me know if he hasn't turned up by the time you get there. Tell Esme I'll call her mother, and get Brian to call her, too, so she's not in the dark." By the time I'd called the law firm and lined up Brian and a senior associate to go to the station with him, and then spent five minutes on the phone with Maggie vainly attempting to allay her anxiety with spotty information, and left a message on Jennifer's phone, twenty minutes of meeting time had gone by.

When I walked back into the boardroom, everyone was fidgety and fuming. They couldn't start without me because I was designated to make the primary presentation. My face must have looked ghastly because one of my partners stood up and stared at me, and one of the oil executives demanded, "My good God, Mr. McGill, are you all right?"

What was I supposed to say? Oh yes, I'm fine, it's just that my teenaged niece has been charged with a drug-related murder and my daughter will probably be charged as an accessory to murder. Did credentials for a lawyer trying to get retained by uptight corporate types get any better than that? I apologized for the delay and told them the truth, a strictly technical truth: The seventeen-year-old daughter of a client of the firm, which Maggie was, had gotten herself mixed up in a drug bust and an allegation of murder, I said, and I had to make sure of proper representation by someone qualified in the firm back home. I told them that the timing was unfortunate, but I considered attending to the matter to be a higher priority, frankly, than starting our meeting on time.

My partners looked down and said nothing, probably suspecting the fuller truth. The CEO said, "You did the right thing, Bill. There but for the grace of God go I—go all of us." He looked around at the nodding heads. Each of them must have had teenaged kids or grandchildren out of control or tending that way.

We began our presentation and, to be honest, if immodest, I outdid myself. My desire to make up for the wasted time, and to blank out whatever nightmare was mushrooming back home, concentrated my mind wonderfully, and I could feel that we were making a very positive impression on the group.

Afterwards, the CEO said he found my judgment call on the relative importance of a personal catastrophe of a client, compared with getting the meeting going, to be notable. It showed the kind of solid wisdom and acumen that, as a human being and a parent and grandparent, he wanted a piece of. Corporate heads nodded. Lawyerly faces beamed. With our firm solidly retained, I marvelled over the ironic quirk: my sought-after success was at least partly caused by an adversity that I would not have wished on that guy in grade eight who'd deliberately tripped me in soccer and broke my leg.

I rushed down to get a taxi back to the hotel, where I could lock myself in my room and plumb the depths by telephone of this fresh upheaval in our family life. On the way, my mind brought back the location of the crime Molly had mentioned. Near Windsor Lake. Lots of the drug trafficking seemed to take place just outside the city, and Windsor Lake, a reservoir fifteen minutes away from the city, with no houses close to it and with trails leading into the woods hidden from prying law-enforcement eyes, was a perfect spot for it. So, at the time, I thought nothing else about the locale.

CHAPTER seven

I reached Brian Keeping by phone in his car outside the police station. He'd just finished meeting with the investigating detectives and the girls. First in line had been Molly. They had kept her in a small room by herself, seated at a table. A detective told Brian that they didn't have a handle yet on what she'd been doing out there in the car. She might have just been innocently along for the ride with the other one or she might be somehow involved, either in the drug purchase or the murder, or both.

They weren't charging her with anything at the moment, but that could change fast. They'd see what their investigation brought forward. Meanwhile, they were releasing her into the custody of her mother on the condition that she wouldn't leave town and would be available at any time for more questioning.

A female constable wondered out loud, said Brian, why parents would give seventeen-year-old girls the dangerous independence and freedom of owning their own car. What do moms and dads expect, she asked her partner, but mischief and foul play from such permissive, overindulgent spoiling of their kids? Molly told them her mom and dad had bought the old second-hand car for her and Esme because Esme's mother was paralyzed and the girls picked up her groceries and medications and other shopping with it.

The officers were unmoved. One of them nodded and said sarcastically, rolling his eyes, "Oh, of course, you certainly need a car these days for shopping for dope for your paralyzed mother."

The cops seemed very hard-nosed, said Brian, and frankly he would not be surprised if Molly were to be charged with, as one of them put it, being at least an accessory to murder—to wit, the driver of the getaway car—and maybe even an accomplice. Brian told the police that I was Molly's father and Esme's guardian, since her father was dead and her mother nearly quadriplegic. On hearing that, the police exchanged a look of what could only be described as satisfaction. They'd lucked onto a good one. Not as good as, say, the premier's or the lieutenant-governor's daughter, perhaps, but still a nice medium-sized fish hefty enough to make a noticeable splash, and to emphasize to the public their zero tolerance of drugs, no matter who was involved, the low or the high.

When they brought in Esme, Brian said, they had her in leg shackles and handcuffs. He'd protested, saying, "Surely that's not necessary."

"Absolutely and totally necessary," said one of the officers. "Last week a sixteen-year-old girl we had in custody for breaking into a house and robbing an elderly lady in her own bed at knifepoint bolted out of the police car on the way to court and fled on foot. It took us three days to find her again. We've had egg all over our faces on the open-line shows ever since. You can imagine the uproar if someone accused of a drug-related murder vamoosed on us."

Brian recounted to me the story so far that he'd pieced together from the detectives and Esme and Molly. The police had received a 911 call from Esme on her cell saying she was down a trail off Old Broad Cove Road next to Windsor Lake and there was a man there who looked like he was dead. A sharp stick or broken branch or something must have gone into his eye, she said. They asked if she was in any danger while they got directions from her about where she was parked, and told her to stay put in the car and lock the doors and they'd dispatch a patrol car right away.

When the police car got there a few minutes later, the two constables saw two civilian cars parked at the entrance to the trail. A young man was hurriedly getting into one; he took off in it when he saw the police car turning in, but the officer got the licence number and called it in.

The other car contained Esme and Molly. Esme led the officers down the trail a short way to a small natural clearing where they saw a man in his twenties lying on the ground. The police felt for a pulse and then proclaimed him deceased. It looked as if his brain had been pierced through his eye, one officer said, but they could see nothing near him, a stick or knife or the like, which might have done it.

Esme told the officers that the victim, whose name was Jason, had sold her marijuana down by the lake. She didn't know him but she'd seen him before in a car parked a short distance from the school. Some boys in her class, who were with her when she'd asked about him, called him the Candyman, and she'd approached him and made the arrangements to meet.

When Esme and Jason had completed their transaction near the lake, she started to walk back to the car, but he put his arm around her chest from behind. He made an obscene suggestion as to what they could do "down here all alone like this," and he offered her a free Desoxyn tablet "to get you goin'."

She was able to twist and shrug him off, and then she threatened to scream and stab him with the hiking pole she had strapped to her wrist. To make her point, she actually thrust the point of her pole down into his boot. Jason swore, apparently in pain, and backed off. He said, "Don't worry, I'll get you yet. I always do." Brian said to me that it would have been better if Esme hadn't told the police any of that—it provided them with a half-baked motive they could fixate on, and brought attention to her lethal pole.

Esme's story continued: after Jason let her go, and she was about to walk back to the car, he told her to tell the guy in the other car that he'd be there in a minute—first he had to use the bathroom.

"Was that the word he used, 'bathroom'?" an officer asked.

"No, he said 'take a leak,'" replied Esme, and the officer told her to use the words Jason used.

They were already near the water, but he stepped to the very edge of the shore and started to pull down his fly. According to Esme, she said to him, "My God, you're not going to do that right in the lake; that's the city's drinking water."

Jason replied, "Yeah, like I gives a sweet shag about a bunch of townies drinking my pee. Looks good on them."

"And no, 'pee' wasn't the exact word he used," Esme told her questioner.

Esme had turned away from Jason and walked quickly on, keeping him in her peripheral vision. Next she heard some sort of a squawk, and then, before she had a chance to turn around completely, she glimpsed, out of the corner of her eye, something large flying through the air. It seemed to be moving higher than her height, and when she turned and focused on it, she saw it was Jason. He landed on the ground by some trees about ten or twelve feet from the shoreline.

She waited for him to move, and when he didn't, she went over to him. He wasn't stirring. His eye looked punctured and there was blood everywhere. When she called his name and prodded him with her toe and then with her pole, there was absolutely no movement or response.

She ran to the car, got in, and told Molly what had happened. The guy in the other car jumped out and shouted, "Whassup? What's going down?" or words equally cool, and jogged down the trail. A few minutes later, he came flying back, swearing and bawling, and was running at the girls' car with fury in his eyes when he heard a police siren. He hopped back in his own car and started it. The police arrived just as his car was pulling out. Soon Esme and Molly heard another police car rush by, its siren wailing.

They caught the other guy, whose name was Danny Power, the brother of the victim, and found his car loaded with hashish and hard drugs—oxycodone pills, Percocet, Desoxyn, cocaine, ecstasy, you name it. Jason Power, the dead man, had a variety of drugs on his person, too. Esme and Molly had nothing on them and there were no drugs in their car. Esme had thrown her bag of grass into the woods as she was running to the car. The police quickly found the ditched bag.

It might have been better if she'd kept it on her, said Brian, as now the police were claiming she must have bought harder drugs, too, which she'd also ditched somewhere. They kept asking her what she'd done with the hard stuff. Had she thrown it in the lake?

At this point, Brian told me, Esme's mother, Maggie, showed up at the station. She'd managed to get Wheelway, the transportation service for people with disabilities, to bring her there at short notice. She told the police that it was all her fault, that she had talked Esme against her will into buying marijuana for her in order to curb the muscle spasms she was suffering.

Esme said that wasn't true. It was she who had seen an article on the Internet about medical marijuana being used for that purpose and she had suggested it to her mother, who turned it down flat. Her mother had told her, Esme said, that she couldn't drag her brother, Bill, him being a lawyer, into that kind of thing by spending his money on dope. Her mother had also told Esme that she was going to mention marijuana therapy to her doctor on the next visit, although she doubted he'd go along with it. Esme and Molly decided something had to be done, and, like a dutiful daughter and niece, they did it on their own. It was all her own idea, though, said Esme. Molly had nothing to do with it.

The police exhibited skepticism over both stories—mother's and daughter's. Hadn't Esme already been thrown out of school at least once for toking up in the washroom? It appeared, said Brian, that the principal had reported that incident. And in any event, the detectives said, matters had proceeded far beyond any defence claim of innocently purchasing marijuana for medical purposes, and even beyond any police allegation of purchase for the purpose of trafficking. This was a case of murder, perpetrated during the commission of an indictable offence.

Preliminary lab tests showed that there was blood on Esme's hiking pole, which she had tried to scrape off on moss, evidently; police suspected that it was the victim's. DNA tests would no doubt confirm that. There was no uncertainty in their minds that Esme had stabbed him in the eye with her pole. She had already used the pole to attack a fox. That charge, though withdrawn, was still in her police file, too.

Now ordinarily, the police said, they might have been justified in charging Esme with just manslaughter, and perhaps her lawyer could argue self-defence as a result of the victim's alleged attempted assault on her. But in this case, the homicide took place during the commission of a serious crime, thereby requiring that the charge be second-degree murder.

Moreover, because the chief of police and the Department of Justice, and the premier herself, had made it clear publicly that there was to be no tolerance shown to perpetrators, young and old alike, in the escalating drug scene that was part of the booming St. John's economy, the prosecution would be applying to the judge to have Esme, who'd be eighteen on her next birthday, and was possessed of mature intelligence, tried as an adult.

They seemed determined, said Brian, to make her into an example, and she was ideal for the purpose—good family, good grades, good character—not some lout from whom nothing better could be expected. The traumatic death of her father and her mother's infirmity added to her status as a poster child for the war on dope. It proved that no one was immune from involvement with drugs. This arrest would proclaim loud and clear to young people of all stations and conditions in life that the justice system was demonstrating zero tolerance to all drug perpetrators.

And if Esme were to be found guilty of second-degree murder as an adult, which was the likely outcome according to the police, she would be sentenced to life in prison with no chance of parole for fifteen years or more. However, if her lawyers were inclined to spare everybody the cost and inconvenience of a full-fledged trial by having her simply confess to killing Jason Power, no doubt a better deal might be worked out for her. There were no guarantees, but a guilty plea to manslaughter might net her, for example, only a ten-year sentence, or perhaps less.

"If Esme were to be tried as an adult," I said to Brian, "her identity would automatically be made public and her life and career chances would be ruined, whether she was found innocent or guilty. How do you assess the position the police are taking?"

"Bill, it doesn't look all that good. They are really gung-ho to nail her as an example. There's no doubt about that. I heard them say what a piece of luck it was that you, this big corporate lawyer, were related to Esme and Molly."

"What are they going to do about Molly, do you think?"

"They're playing coy on that at the moment, but I'd be extremely surprised if they didn't do their worst."

"Okay, apply for bail for Esme right away. Let's retain the best criminal lawyer in town to lead us in handling this. Confer with senior members of our firm on that and call me with the recommendations. No reflection on you, Brian, but only on your age and experience."

"I agree. The cops were treating me like a rank amateur in there. There's no one senior in the firm who's really up to speed on this stuff. If they're going to try her as an adult for murder, we definitely need to hit them with someone high-powered."

CHAPTER eight

I was scheduled to have lunch and dinner with the executives and lawyers in Calgary the next day. Before I talked to Brian, I had decided I would stay despite the ruckus at home. After all, there was nothing I could accomplish on the spot, personally, regarding the immediate judicial procedures. They were best left in the hands of lawyers who knew what they were doing, and they could consult with me by phone. But Brian's report on Esme's description of the place and manner of the victim's death had gripped my mind, and I could think of nothing else. I telephoned my regrets to my partners and our client for having to leave, called the airline, cancelled the flight home I'd reserved, and booked the red-eye for that evening.

Mostly sleepless, I flew from Calgary to Toronto to Halifax to St. John's, arriving at the airport at midday feeling overwrought and agitated. I didn't even go home first. I'd called Brian from Toronto, waking him up early in the morning, to tell him to meet me at the airport, and to bring Molly with him. We were going to drive straight to the place near the lake where Esme and Molly had parked their car. I'd called Jennifer and Maggie from Halifax to confirm my plan.

When she saw me at the baggage carousel, Molly charged ahead of Brian and put her arms around me. I was struck by the contrast between how mature and womanly she had started to look this year and the little girl's face on her as she held onto me tight and whispered how sorry she was. I murmured, "Shh, we'll talk in the car."

As we drove the few miles to the lake, I said, "Molly, we're not going to get into any guilty-innocent, good-evil analysis of this. The whole thing is mind-boggling, yes, but remember that whatever happens, your mother and I will love you as much whether you're behind bars in prison or winning a scholarship to Harvard. Now where were you parked, exactly?"

Nearing that place, we saw an empty police vehicle. We pulled in, parked, and got out of the car, and Molly led us to the opening of the trail. The grass and brush were wet under our feet. As we entered the woods, we met two uniformed police officers, a male and a female, on their way up. They told us to stop; we were not allowed near the crime site. I told them that we were the girls' lawyers, and we had to look at the place where these two young female teenagers had supposedly committed the Criminal Code's most serious crime. The policewoman called through to her superior, who said the site was off limits; the prosecution would be sharing with the defence any evidence that supported either side of the case.

I said, loudly, "Please tell him that it has already rained since the alleged crime took place and we need to look at the site before any further evidence is destroyed or made useless by the elements." I raised my voice more, my temper ballooning. "Tell him he's making this very easy for us: our next step will be to apply to a judge for dismissal of the charges because of obstruction of justice by the police."

Brian touched my arm: Don't lose it. And evidently, the supervisor, as well as the police officers, knew the sound of a crazed lawyer when they heard it, one who would make no end of trouble. The policewoman listened to her phone in silence for twenty seconds, eyeballing me unkindly the whole while, and then said, "Yes, sir, I agree. I would." She listened again, and then explained their decision to me. "You are to proceed to the 'do not cross' tape and survey the site from there. Under no circumstances are you to enter or act in such manner as to contaminate the crime scene. Anything further will require a court order. Are we clear on the conditions?"

"Entirely." We walked down to the tape. Another police officer was standing near a tent covering a few square metres of ground by some trees. "Is that where the body was found?" I asked.

"Affirmative."

We could scarcely hear ourselves. The crows were cawing in an unusually strident manner from the trees near the water where they had gathered in numbers greater than I'd ever seen in one place, except perhaps once before.

One of the policemen waved an arm at them and said, "They've been here since yesterday. They must be mad at us for moving the body they had their greedy little eyes on. I hate crows."

The last time I'd heard them this loud and in such numbers was when I'd seen the tentacle grab the gull. Were they agitated like this by yesterday's event in this spot, just as they had been by the event two decades ago? Their raucous presence here again today was evidence of nothing, but the crows were helping to give me the gut feeling that Esme's story and my sighting back then were both part of the same "truth."

I looked out across the lake. Seagulls were markedly absent from the surface of the water. In my youth we used to joke that the gulls—we called them rats with wings—would dine in their hundreds on the garbage at the city dump at Robin Hood Bay and then flock over here to the drinking water supply to rinse the filth off their dainty, protected-species little feet. In recent years, though, they seemed to have largely abandoned the lake.

I scanned the spruce trees that stood behind the tent in a straight line from the lake. About eight feet up on the foremost tree I could see a broken-off branch projecting rigidly out from the trunk some five or six inches. Perhaps it was my lack of sleep, plus anxiety from contemplating the possible futures of two lovely, bright, blundering young women, that stimulated my imagination: I saw plainly in my mind's eye a young man standing by the water's edge urinating into the lake, and then I saw with absolute clarity his offending body being flung by some immense unknown force across the glade to the tree and its eye-impaling branch. And I saw his body drop to the ground. My heart sank as I looked at the droplets of rainwater on the vegetation and realized that overnight showers might have already washed away crucial evidence, or it might have been eaten by the crows.

I pointed out the tree to Brian, and asked if he could see the broken branch. He could, and confirmed its height, length, and colouring. "Do whatever is necessary," I went on, "either through the police or by court order, to have the forensic people collect anything adhering to or around that branch and the trunk of the tree under it, and have it analyzed and identified in a lab."

"Uh, okay. It's two feet or more higher than the height of a man. What do you expect to find?"

"Human blood and brain. And do it quickly, before we have another downpour of rain or feast of crows."

Brian Keeping, my own legal associate, was the first to give me that odd, curious look I would grow accustomed to from everyone before this case ended, the look that asked: Has the strain driven this poor fellow around the bend?

With co-operation from the police, people from the lab scraped the branch and the bark on the trunk and found organic matter on the underside of the branch and directly below it—blood and brain matter—identified as human, and then, with further testing, as belonging to the victim, Jason Power.

CHAPTER nine

At our meeting with the prosecution and police about the evidence scraped from the tree, they pronounced themselves unimpressed. How could that material have possibly gotten up there, they asked, if it wasn't scraped off the end of her hiking pole by Esme? She was easily tall enough to reach the branch with her pole, and when she'd first noticed the fortuitously placed broken branch above the body, the clever girl concocted her bizarre story and did what was necessary to support it.

"But she didn't say anything to you about that branch, did she?" I asked. "It wasn't even part of her so-called 'concocted story.'"

"No, her uncle came in with that part for us," said the Crown prosecutor, Derek Smythe. "The old one-two punch. Oh, it's all very cute and everything. But perhaps too cute by half."

Brian leaned over and whispered to me, "Uh, Mr. McGill, maybe it would be best if you left this to me and Mr. Sheppard.

He'll be here in a minute." He was referring to highly esteemed criminal lawyer Morley Sheppard, Q.C., whom we had retained. My protégé then added a word of caution to me, his mentor, older than him by twenty years: "You may be a bit too emotionally close to the girls." It was the first time I'd heard "emotionally close" used as a euphemism for "wacky." But it told me that I'd be going mostly solo in my quest for answers to Esme's eerie mystery.

First I talked alone to Esme at the juvenile detention centre where they were holding her. I had her repeat what happened at the time of Jason Power's death. Had she seen anything out in the lake before or during the squawk she thought she'd heard from him?

"No, nothing, Uncle Bill, but I wasn't looking. I was too busy fending him off and then getting away from him as quick as I could."

"Did you hear anything besides the noise you think he made?"

"I'm tempted to say I heard a loud sound of water on the rocks, like some big waves were hitting them, but I'm not sure. Before, or maybe at the same time as he was flying through the air, I think I heard a 'whoosh' sound of some kind. But that's very vague in my mind.

"One thing that's extremely clear in my memory, though, is the fact that he did fly through the air. Last year I watched this horrible documentary on TV about dwarf-tossing—men throwing a dwarf in a Velcro suit up against a Velcro wall—and, it's awful for me to say it, but that's exactly what it seemed like with him, Jason, except he had no helmet or protection on. It was like he was a dwarf being tossed by a strong man."

"Is it possible he jumped or leaped in some way?"

"No, not possible, Uncle Bill. He came flying across. But I know nobody will believe my story and I don't blame them. It's too totally weird."

I was about to tell Esme about what I'd seen out on the lake over two decades ago, but I decided not to. Not yet. I didn't want to give her any "factual" information of a similar nature that might bolster her imagination, or raise false hopes. I did say, though, "I believe you, Esme. But I need to explore the possibilities, independently, a little more."

CHAPTER ten

I had acted for a client, John Tucker, a couple of years before, whose grandfather wanted to deed over to him his house on Old Broad Cove Road, near Windsor Lake. The grandfather, Mr. Hughie Tucker, had lived there all his life, but now wanted to move into a nursing home. His wife had recently died, he loved company, and he had no wish to live with any of his three children, all of whom had made it clear how much they loved the empty nest syndrome they were suffering from, now that all their darlings had left home.

John Tucker, my client, was Hughie's eldest grandchild and I got the impression he was the only one who paid much attention to the old guy. He wanted me to go to his grandfather and advise him that it was best to sell the house and keep the money himself, or divide it up evenly among his children. "I don't want my aunt and uncle and my own father sending a hit man over my way," he said. "Or, at best, all of them going to court to say Pop is of unsound mind. They always claimed he's more than a bit peculiar with his old foolishness."

I told John I couldn't advise his grandfather because of a conflict of interest. If old Mr. Tucker still wanted to give the house to his grandson after getting my advice, other family members might claim undue influence. It would be in everybody's best interests for the old man to have absolutely independent legal advice.

That was done, but old Mr. Tucker still insisted on giving the house to John. I was glad about it, because I wanted to be present at the signing over, and casually ask the old man afterwards if, in his long memory, he'd ever seen or heard of anything odd and inexplicable in Windsor Lake.

To make it easier to get to Hughie Tucker's hard-to-find house, the three of us—my client, John, the other lawyer, Steve Jenkins, and I—drove out together. Hughie met us at the gate, spry and twinkle-eyed, and obviously sharp as a tack.

After he'd executed the deed presented to him by Jenkins at the kitchen table, he sat back and said, "This is my best shot at keeping the house in the family for a while. It's over a hundred years old, and there's been some wonderful creepy old yarns told right here in this room."

This was my chance to ask for some examples of yarns concerning the lake, but before I could open my mouth, the old man jumped up and went out to the adjoining porch. There he opened a large tool box and lifted off the top layer of screwdrivers and pliers. "To mark the occasion," he said, pulling out from the lower compartment a bottle of dark rum. "I know that my grandson is driving, so I'll go easy on him."

Into three tumblers he splashed about three ounces of liquor each. Less than an ounce went into the fourth. "I was married fifty-six years and my wife never knew, first nor last, that there was a bottle of this in that box." He pushed the tumblers toward us—no ice, no mix, no water. "Okay, b'ys," he said, lifting his own glass in salute. "Go mad."

"There was a downside, though, Pop," John said. "You wouldn't let Nan touch your tool box. No wife of yours, you said, was lifting a hand to do men's work. So, if a doorknob was loose, or a picture had to be hung on a nail, or a carpet tack was sticking up, she wasn't allowed to do it. Only you could get a screwdriver or hammer out and attend to the job."

"Yes, and she always thought I was doing it all myself, and stopping her from doing it, all because of love. So, no downside there, sonny. I got an awful lot of mileage out of that, on top of me few swallies of this. She treated me like King George." His eyes started to overflow. "Sorry," he sniffed. "I was supposed to go first, and she was supposed to do all this shagging mourning." He sniffed again and drank. "My big challenge now is to make sure I can get myself a drink now and then at that home."

"I'll fix that up," said John. "Don't worry about that."

I jumped in with the question that had brought me out here. "Mr. Tucker, Windsor Lake up there. There's not much human activity on or near it. So the trout must be able to grow pretty big there, I suppose. Have you ever seen or heard of any large fish, or any other creature, for that matter, living in the lake?"

"Windsor Lake? A bunch over on Portugal Cove Road pushed

for that name years ago. It's too late now, but I still like Twenty Mile Pond, myself. No, can't say I've seen anything unusual there with my own eyes. But there was always stories going around, a lot of cuffers from the olden days. Old foolishness, I'd say."

I asked if he could tell me one. He was taking a deep breath to begin, when his lawyer Steve Jenkins stood abruptly with a look of panic in his eyes at the thought of an interminable piece of old foolishness coming up. He had to get back to the office right away, he said. He had an appointment in thirty minutes, and he had to stop at a shop en route to get some mints—couldn't have his client thinking he was taking a nip of superior black rum in the middle of the day.

We all had to leave in John's car, so I told Mr. Tucker I'd love to hear his stories and yarns some other time. He'd really look forward to it, he said, and I heard him whispering to his grandson at the door, after Jenkins had gone out, "Next time, get me this other fella for a lawyer, someone who doesn't mind having a little gab for a couple of seconds."

I had always meant to go with John to visit Mr. Tucker at the nursing home and chat to him about Twenty Mile Pond, but legal busywork and a lack of urgency at the time soon put my intentions on the back burner.

Now, a year or more later, in the wake of Esme's experience there, I called John Tucker and asked if his grandfather was still alert and active. "As feisty as ever," he said. "I was in to see him on Sunday. Sure, he called up *Open Line* last week after that power outage and blasted the light and power company for being so useless. This is

Newfoundland, out in the middle of the North Atlantic, he said. When are they going to notice that there's wind and rain and salt-water spray out here every now and again?"

"Sounds like a sensible question to me. Do you think it would be all right if I visited him? I'd like to chat with him for half an hour about something I need to know about Windsor Lake."

"He'd be delighted. He was wondering last year if you ever mentioned to me about following up on that."

"Did you ever solve the black rum challenge he was worried about at the home?"

"Kind of. They keep a bottle for him locked in a drawer under the front desk and dole out an ounce for him before supper. The doctor says that more alcohol than that wouldn't be good for him. Pop said to him, 'I'm eighty-eight. What do you think kept me alive this long?' But no dice. He says the doc is driving him nuts, going by medical science all the time."

"Tell him to remind the doctor what Kingsley Amis said. 'No pleasure is worth giving up for the sake of two more years in a geriatric home.'"

"I will. He'll love that. Meanwhile, the upshot of it all, between ourselves, is that I sneak a flask in now and then. He's got a hiding place. Don't ask me where."

"I'd like to bring one in."

"Good idea. Slip it in with the legal files in your briefcase."

CHAPTER eleven

Hughie Tucker was glad to see me. After we sat down, the first thing he said was, "I told the doctor what that writer said about giving up pleasure, and he comes back, 'Oh Hughie, this is a lovely home and we all want to have you around for as long we can.' My God, a sooky doctor. Is there anything worse?"

I glanced at the door and said, "I told your grandson I wanted to be part of the solution." I opened my briefcase and presented the flask.

"And you are, sir, you are. That was not necessary, but welcome nevertheless." He seized it gently, if an action can be soft but decisive at the same time, and went into his bathroom with it.

"Have you got a good place to hide it? I wouldn't want you to get in their bad books out front because of me."

"Not going to happen, sir. It will be as elusive to searchers as the monster Old Twen."

"The monster?"

"Old Twenny, the monster of Twenty Mile Pond." The hair went up on my neck. "That's what you came to talk about, isn't it? The old foolishness about something horrible in Twenty Mile Pond. When I was growing up, the mothers around there used to say to their kids when they were bad, 'Be good, luh, or I'm going to chuck you in the big pond and Old Twenny will eat you.' Twenny. Twenty Mile Pond, get it?"

"Yep, got it. Where did that monster idea come from? Did a child, to your knowledge, ever get lost around or drowned in Twenty Mile Pond?"

"Never heard of one. It was just something else mothers and fathers dreamed up to keep their kids in line, like the boogeyman, or Satan, or God. If you're bad, the boogeyman will get you, or God will send you down to hell so Satan can roast you on a fire forever, or we'll get Old Twenny to gobble you up. Same sort of nonsense."

"There must have been something, though, that led to the creation of a specific monster in that particular body of water."

"Well, there's a few old yarns and cuffers, and tall tales I used to hear now and then. One had to do with a governor of Newfoundland years ago, I don't know when. The law says that no one is ever allowed to fish on Twenty Mile Pond, the water supply for the city, except for the governor, and only one day a year. A special privilege for the lord high mucky-muck."

"Yes, I read about that."

"So this governor decided to go trouting there with his little nine-year-old granddaughter. One of his servants over from

England hauled a small rowboat out to the pond for the purpose. The servant rowed them out to the middle of the pond, where gramps and the little one flicked their lines about in all directions. They were using worms from the barn manure at Government House, and I was told that at one point the old man, who took a nip, knocked the whole can full of worms and manure overboard into the water. He also didn't like the sandwiches they'd prepared for him—didn't fancy the mustard. 'French!' he bawled out and dumped the whole works into the pond. Now this was the clean drinking water for the citizens we're talking about here. Anyway, as to what happened next, I was told two different versions of by some old-timers around there. Want to hear them?"

"I certainly do, Mr. Tucker."

"Some said that a sudden turbulence sprang up in and over the whole pond, but some said there was a commotion around the boat only. Whatever it was, the boat overturned, throwing all three of them into the water. And the boat sank like a stone. Some said it was wooden and should have floated, but got yanked under; others said there was metal in its construction and it was just too heavy to float upside down. Nobody in the boat, the men or the little girl, had life jackets on—it was way back before these politically correct days. They were hundreds of yards from shore, and the little girl was going to drown for sure, and one or both of the men, too, especially if they spent their strength trying to save her.

"But some eyewitnesses reported seeing the girl out in front of the men, swimming rapidly toward the shore. It was almost as if something unseen, some force, was pushing her along the surface of the water. Others said no, the servant grabbed a hold of the girl and swam toward the shore with her, leaving the old guy to fend for himself. The girl got to shore ahead of the men, they said, because some people on land waded out and took her from the servant, who then went back for the guv. Meanwhile, with help from the bystanders, the two men finally floundered in, half-dead.

"Some said the girl reported that a big fish or something helped her to get in alive. Others said she was referring to the servant, who swam like a big fish and saved her life. Whatever caused the near-disaster and the rescue, the governor banned anyone from mentioning any of it in newspapers or anywhere else, publicly."

"Why do you think he did that, Mr. Tucker?"

"Call me Hughie. Going by my knowledge of human nature, and taking the odd nip myself, I'd say the old geezer was drunk and capsized the boat and nearly drowned his little granddaughter, so the last thing he wanted was anyone asking questions or inquiring too closely. That is, if any of it, in fact, happened at all, which I doubt."

"Why don't you believe any of it, Hughie?"

"Well, sir, you see, I've been saddled all my life with this burden called a brain. All the same, though, what did you think of that old yarn?"

"Very interesting. What else can you tell me?"

"Listen, Mr. McGill . . ."

"Call me Bill, Hughie."

"I do have a couple more old stories about the secrets of Twenty Mile Pond, Bill, good ones, but we'll have to do it on another day.

I've got craft in ten minutes and I've got to get dickied up for the girls."

"Craft? What do you do there?"

"Needlepoint. I'm working on a cushion with a cute little kitten design on it."

Looking at the big robust man with hands on him the size of baseball mitts, I struggled to keep the grin off my face. "Any other men doing needlepoint with you?"

"Not one, Bill, my son. It's okay, though, you can go ahead and laugh. No men? See, that's the beauty of the thing. I'm in there all by myself with the ladies. I've got my eye on this one. She's only seventy-five, but I think she already hinted to me that our age difference is no big deal. 'Thirteen years is not very much,' she said to me one day. She was supposed to be grieving about her last dog, which had just died at that age, before she came in here. But. *But.* It's exactly the same difference between her age and mine. Coincidence? I think not. Sorry to kick you out, but I can't miss craft. Come back again as soon as you get a chance, though."

CHAPTER twelve

At the law office, I asked Brian to track down any references in the public records and old newspapers to governors of Newfoundland fishing on Windsor Lake and any accidents associated therewith, especially if there was a young granddaughter involved.

He looked at me dubiously. "Governors, fishing, granddaughters? Is this relative to the charges against Esme?" After my solemn nod, and under my steady gaze—sane-looking, I hoped—he said, "Well, you never know where any thread may lead us, I guess."

A day or two later, Brian came back with what he'd gleaned from archived journals and papers. He'd found references to a governor in the last quarter of the nineteenth century who'd prematurely departed from Newfoundland after only a few months. He'd been transferred at his own request to a part of India which was then in a state of bloody insurrection. "I wish to go where the Empire needs me most," he was reported as saying.

But, for some unknown reason, the newspaper report seemed skeptical about his motives. It kept referring to his "health" in inverted commas, as in, "It is common knowledge that his Excellency's 'health' has been far from excellent, and many observers locally have frankly wondered whether a man of questionable 'health' ought to be leaving here for obscure reasons to make his presence felt in so hazardous a part of the Empire."

But what really attracted Brian's attention to the piece was the bit on the governor's nine-year-old granddaughter. "The grown-ups, especially Grandpapa, may not agree," she was quoted as saying, "but I shall be truly sorry to leave this enchanted isle, and my friend the water goblin." Her mother explained this reference as originating in the active imagination of a child saddened at their leave-taking.

Brian showed me an anonymous letter to the editor on the day of the governor's departure. It was in the form of a few lines of irregular doggerel. He didn't think it had any relevance to what I was looking for because it seemed meaningless, but since it did refer to the governor in the title, I might spot something useful in it, or at least find it bizarrely amusing. I read it over:

"Our Governor, Well Preserved"
During your stay in our land
Really shorter than planned
Under strain of being the lead
Now take you God's speed.
Keep your fort well manned,

Enough to save worm feed
Now angling's been banned.
For though you had mead
On your table well planned
Oft you paid it too much heed.
Leave us o'erjoyed, we plead.

Brian said, "It's not poetry's greatest moment, is it? And I'm surprised the paper even published it, since it doesn't make a lot of sense."

"You do somewhat get its drift, though, Brian."

"But here's the thing, Bill. Two days later, in the same paper, I saw another letter drawing attention to what was either a remarkable coincidence in the poem or a deliberate but cleverly concealed defamation. I never would have spotted it myself. See it?"

"Oh yes. Oh yes. Look at that. Put together, the first letter of each line spells out two words. I was able to zero in on it because the same thing happened again later in our history, around the time of Confederation. A poem in the paper said goodbye to a governor by spelling out in the same way the words 'the bastard.' And this one here spells out—see it?—'drunken fool.' That's great. It certainly makes the poem relevant to my inquiries. It corroborates an important detail in Mr. Tucker's story about the governor."

On the question of the governors' fishing privilege on Windsor Lake, Brian could not discover any reference to any recent governor having availed himself of the benefit. The go-getter even called up and quizzed the current secretary at Government House, who told him that a tradition had developed there whereby each governor, and every lieutenant-governor since we joined Canada, was advised of a standing policy against doing so because it was too dangerous.

When Brian asked what the danger might be that lay behind that new tradition or policy, the secretary said he didn't know precisely but he suspected—here, Brian said, he could hear the secretary speaking through a grin—that the danger in these more democratic and egalitarian times might have to do with the disastrous public relations inherent in anyone being permitted, simply because of his status, to frolic about in a boat in the people's drinking water.

However, some people, especially the conspiracy theory types, the secretary said, laughing, sometimes darkly hinted that the danger in the lake was more immediate and physical. No, he didn't have any specifics.

CHAPTER thirteen

The very next day, I drove back to see Hughie Tucker, another flask of rum filed away in my briefcase. "You don't have to do that," he said, standing to take the flask, "but thanks all the same." Then he pulled back his hand. "The secret to the success of my hiding place is that it's camouflaged enough to escape notice, like a squid. But if my forbidden loot becomes too noticeable, the whole vast plot may blow up in my face—look, Mr. McGill, Bill, do you mind hanging on to that for me till your next visit? I'll be ready for it then."

"No trouble. How's your needlepoint going?"

"Jackpot, sir. I'm having tea in her room tomorrow afternoon. I'm a bundle of nerves. Haven't closed an eye all night since she asked me. Frightened right to death, trying to keep in mind I'm not supposed to drink my tea out of the saucer. Okay, ready to go? This next yarn about Old Twenny is more recent.

"There was a fellow who used to live on Old Broad Cove Road

not far from me who called himself the Multi-Million Dollar Man. He nicknamed himself that because over half his forty-odd years had been spent in prison for assorted crimes. Twenty-five years at eighty grand a year, which is what he calculated it cost the government in police work, and trials, and to put him up in the clink—'Well, do the math,' he'd say, right proud of himself. The Multi-Million Dollar Man.

"He might have seemed like an idiot, but one time he was in court, with twelve different charges against him—car theft, bank heist, breaking into a house to hide out, assault on a gang member who ratted on him, a shootout with the RCMP, the list goes on. He turned down the legal aid lawyer and defended himself. He got nine of the twelve charges thrown out by the judge."

"I remember that case," I said. "He was the darling of the media, never stopped crowing about how he'd made a fool of the entire league of legal beagles in the province. A bunch of us lawyers were talking about it at the time, and one, a senior criminal lawyer, said, 'That guy must be a genius. I've been following the trial and I'll tell you straight: I doubt if I could have gotten all of those nine charges dismissed.'"

"There you go," said Hughie. "And I'm telling you that part of it now because, when you hear what happened at the end, you need to keep in mind that the man was far from a moron. The Multi-Million Dollar Man was very active, very energetic. I think half his problem was his hyperactivity. He should have been prime minister or a big business magnate where his insane energy and his criminal tendencies could have done him a lot more good.

"After he got out of jail the last time, he decided he was going to hike around Twenty Mile Pond. Now he'd done it before, but he wanted to break his own record. The time before, he took about seven and a half hours to do it, over the bogs, rocks, and through the thick underbrush. This time, he bragged, he was going to break seven hours. So he and his gang of disciples took off from the starting point like scalded cats.

"Two or three hours later, when they were over on the side of the lake where there's no regular road, he told the boys he had to use the bathroom. 'You guys go on ahead,' he said. 'I won't have any trouble catching up with all you snails and slugs.' He was standing right by the lake on the beach, undoing his belt, and one of his buddies said, 'You're not going to take a dump there, are you? My uncle is in the pen in town and he has to drink that water.' And Multi says, 'Then he should be happy. This will be an improvement over what they used to serve me when I was inside.' The boys all laughed and went on their way, saying what a queer hand old Multi was. And they never saw the man again. Nobody did. There and then, he disappeared off the very face of the earth.

"One of his gang of hikers told the police that he heard something behind him, not enough to make him turn his head, sort of a 'yip.' A sound like a dog might make if it was run over by a truck and killed instantly. Or like a man might make if his neck was suddenly broken. The descriptions rang true, the police said, because the boys gave every impression of being comfortably familiar with terminal sounds.

"Three scenarios were put forward. The first two were proposed by the police.

"First, they suggested the possibility of suicide, since he was about to be brought up on habitual offender charges. But they never really pursued that. As his girlfriend said to them, 'Multi? Commit suicide? Multi causes suicide, he don't do suicide.'

"The second possibility, and the one the police really favoured, was that his own buddies murdered him. He always had a big mouth, but it kept getting worse, and God alone knew what he would say to a jailhouse informant when he got going, not to intentionally rat on the boys, but just to shoot off his face. So the theory was that some of his gang wanted to shut him up permanently.

"The police dragged the bottom of the pond in the area where he was last seen, and nothing turned up. They interrogated his companions endlessly. Where had they hidden the body after they killed him? That sort of thing. No one gave an answer and no charges were ever laid. He became a missing person, an eternally missing person. But the police made it clear to the boys that they had gotten away with murder.

"The Department of Justice played down the whole story, especially that a body was never found, because the lack of a body meant it might still be out there in the pond, somewhere on the bottom, weighted down with chains and mouldering away in the city's drinking water. And now we come to scenario number three.

"His death and disappearance, some people claimed, including Multi's own gang, were the handiwork of the monster of Twenty Mile Pond. Only old Twenny was frightening and mysterious and sneaky and powerful enough to kill the great Multi-Million Dollar Man and make him vanish without trace."

"What do you think happened to him, Hughie?"

"Remember I told you how cute and clever he was? I think Multi made himself disappear. I'd say he's been living ever since under an assumed name, probably in a disguise, in some foreign country without an extradition treaty."

"Has there ever been a report that he's been spotted or heard from?"

"No, never, not a sound that I know of."

"But don't you think that's strange, Hughie? Especially since the self-proclaimed Multi-Million Dollar Man craved publicity all his life before that. You'd think he'd be calling or emailing from Uruguay or somewhere like that, giving our justice system the finger and bragging his head off."

"Yes, even his girlfriend used to say she half-expected to see him on television in South America someday, going, 'Yah yah yah yah YAH yah.' Which didn't happen, as far as I know, so I suppose he could be dead."

"Maybe he was, in fact, killed by something in the water and dragged off."

"Maybes are two cents a quintal, Bill. Keep in mind that the ones really pushing the monster idea were the ones who might be able to say, if they were tortured enough, that he was alive and where he escaped to, or that they were the ones who murdered him."

"I suppose," I said. "What about family and belongings? Any indication that persons close to him or things valuable to him disappeared afterwards, too? Some hint that someone went with him or joined him, or that he took some things with him?"

"I was hoping you wouldn't ask me that. Because that's the main thing that casts doubt on my theory that he hightailed to a foreign country. He had his girlfriend here and a couple of children by her that he doted on. And by all accounts he and she doted on each other.

"I remember one time, after nine fellow inmates up in Dorchester Penitentiary, or maybe it was Kingston—he was in a good many jails—anyway, these nine convicts attacked him in the workout room with shanks and shivs and ten-pound cast-iron dumbbells. And he walked out, leaving every one of them a twitching heap of blood and pulp on the floor. Well, sir, the girlfriend comes right on television, and says, 'It'll take more than nine or ten Canadians brandishing lethal weaponry'—she had all the police lingo down pat—'to put down my man.'

"She was heartbroken when he disappeared. You couldn't fake that kind of grief, her mother said. And she never went out of the province after. Afraid of flying. It's pretty certain she never travelled anywhere to visit him. And he never took anything with him. All his belongings were exactly the same as they were before he disappeared."

"What about the kids, did they ever travel anywhere after?"

"Not while they were growing up. They never left the area. One of them is married and living in Fort McMurray now. The other one is in and out of jail—break and enter, holdups, that sort of a thing. He was trying to supplement the family income, I suppose. The girlfriend went on welfare after Multi vanished, and stayed on it until the day she died of cancer a couple of years ago. I'll say this in favour of the monster theory, though: Multi never would have let his family go on welfare like that if he was alive. He always prided himself on providing for them, even while he was in prison. But then, the way he was, you know, if he decided he was going to disappear, he'd well and truly disappear."

"All very strange." We sat and cogitated for a few minutes. Then I said, "Hughie, the lake must have a lot of trout in it by now. Between ourselves, is there much poaching going on there, to your knowledge?"

"Nah. Everyone is too skittish from the foolish old yarns to go out in a small boat, or to even fish from the shore, especially after dark in the middle of the night, when the poaching would have to be done to avoid being caught. I wouldn't be surprised if the city council or the government keeps the legend alive to prevent people going near the water."

"Must be a monster's dream by now, all those big fish. Want to sneak out in a boat some night and catch a couple?"

"I definitely would have gone out with you last month, Bill, when I had no responsibilities, except myself. But someone else's happiness is starting to depend on me now." He grinned and got to his feet. "Listen, Bill, I'm going to mosey out to the TV room to see if there's anyone watching the story, wink, wink, nudge, nudge, if you get my meaning. Next time you come I've got something else to tell you about all this. Now don't think you've got to bring a flask every time you drop in. A full bottle, a twenty-six-ouncer, to put under the desk out there for my nightly medicinal dose would be good sometimes, too. Ha ha ha. Just joking."

CHAPTER fourteen

Molly was charged with being an accessory before and after the fact to second-degree murder and released into the custody of Jennifer and me. The young lady was only lucky, prosecutor Derek Smythe told Morley Sheppard, that she hadn't been charged as an accomplice to murder.

Danny Power, the man who'd been waiting in the car for his brother, the victim, was charged with possession of narcotics for the purpose of trafficking. The Crown waged a rancorous legal battle to keep him in jail. He'd ended up in British Columbia a couple of years ago, they argued, after he'd been charged and released on bail in St. John's. But ultimately, after weeks of wrangling, the judge let him out when he and his sureties made a large deposit, which, the media reported, they appeared to have no problem raising quickly. Among the conditions of his release was an undertaking to have absolutely no contact with Esme and

Molly. That requirement shouldn't have given us as great a sense of security as it did.

Esme's application for bail was difficult, too. A full-scale hearing was held wherein the prosecutor described her as dangerous to the public. He strenuously urged that she be kept in custody until the trial—many months down the road. Now I could understand that the Crown had adopted this hard-nosed attitude as part of the Department of Justice's zero-tolerance policy in drug cases generally, let alone those associated with allegations of murder, but the zeal of the prosecution went way beyond that policy. It seemed to me to be approaching abuse of process. It was almost as if they had some sort of hidden agenda.

Our lawyers, Brian and Morley, however, told me that the police and prosecution were simply irritated by Esme's cockamamie, hare-brained story, and they were counting on a few months in closed custody to bring her to her senses and her account a little closer to reality.

They wanted her either to take responsibility herself or point her finger at Danny Power and give evidence that he had committed the homicide in a scrap over money. Yes, you heard right, Morley said—murdered his own brother, Jason. The Crown had seen cases before where drug money was thicker than blood. They well understood Esme's and Molly's fear of reprisal, of course, if they informed on the brother, but the police would provide protective custody if the girls did the right thing.

In court, the judge, Susan White, listened with a poker face to the prosecutor's final arguments against granting Esme bail, all the while eyeing her, Maggie, Jennifer, and me. Then she heard a little of our lawyer Morley's demolition of the Crown's case, and stopped him mid-argument.

After years of being exposed to this stuff, she hinted, she could pretty well tell that Esme was not a low-life fly-by-night bail jumper. Judge White released her immediately into the joint custody of her mother and me and my wife. Her preliminary hearing on the second-degree murder charge was slated to go ahead in the spring of the next year.

After the bail hearing, when Jennifer and I were driving home by ourselves, she said to me, "The prosecution certainly seems convinced that Esme is guilty."

"Yeah, let's hope their enthusiasm is not contagious at the trial."

"Do you think she's innocent?"

"I think she is, but I don't know. I'm going to act as if she is. Her homicidal monster lurking in the pond theory is hard for people to accept, I realize, but thank God I can get my mind around it because of that similar experience I had there—well, not similar, but of a nature to indicate there's something going on out there. For the two of us, Esme and me, to have had such an experience cannot be just a coincidence. The odds against that would be astronomical."

"Unless she knew of your sighting and then contrived her own little story to dovetail with yours."

"But nobody knew but me. Did you know?"

"No, not until you mentioned it after they charged her. Are you sure you didn't tell anyone, though, just in passing or as a joke, even? What about Maggie?"

It was, as they say, a good question. "You know, Jennifer, I really can't answer that, because I don't remember. It's possible. She was my confidante in everything else, and I was going through agony from my breakup with Ramona."

"The other angle," said Jennifer, "is that, if you in fact told no one at the time, and if there's no one to confirm that you told them at the time, you yourself could easily have made it up now as corroboration of Esme's story after she came up with it. So it cuts both ways. If she made it up, you could have then made up your story to corroborate hers. If she knew of your story, hers could have been modelled on yours."

"Which means neither story is much of a corroboration of the other and might easily be destroyed in court. But maybe some of the other stuff I'm starting to dredge up might support her. What about you? Do you think she's innocent?"

"It may be pure faith, but whatever happened down by the lake that day, I do think she's innocent of murder. I'm just playing devil's advocate here. I can't help thinking of what you would do to me if I were alleging what Esme and you are alleging, and you were cross-examining me about it on the stand."

"Hoard up past resentments a bit, do you, Jen?" We both laughed and she placed her head on my shoulder.

CHAPTER fifteen

On an excuse, I made an appointment with the engineer in charge of the water supply and its treatment for the city. His name was Lancelot Yeo. He had immigrated here from England many years ago, and was inordinately proud of the purity of the water he'd been responsible for ever since.

I had a convenient client whose file was dormant. Last year, he had wanted to sue the city because, he said, his tap water stank. After investigation, I'd been persuaded he had no case and I encouraged him to get his pipes checked and save himself a lot of money by not going up against city hall.

I told Lancelot Yeo that the information I wanted on the quality of his water was off the record and without prejudice. I just wanted to confirm what I'd already satisfied myself about, namely, that there was no basis to my client's complaint that the city was responsible for a smell of algae in his water.

"Shouldn't I have the city solicitor here?" he asked.

"By all means if you wish," I replied. "But that would force me to go to court for an order to produce documents and reports and all the attendant publicity."

"All right, then, let's hear what you want to know."

"What is the quality of the water from Windsor Lake like before it enters the treatment plant and gets chlorinated?"

"Amazingly clean, clear, and pure," said Mr. Yeo. "The raw water in the other reservoir, Bay Bulls Big Pond, is already excellent, too, but not as good as Windsor Lake. It makes no difference, of course, because both supplies ultimately come out of their treatment plants identical in quality. I think perhaps the lake is so pure because it's a geological depression, not fed by surface streams or rivers, and its only recharge is by way of precipitation and groundwater from springs at the bottom. One of our new technicians said, after he'd taken his first sample, that it's almost as if something is out there keeping it clean."

I took a sip of the coffee he'd given me. "Why? Has anyone ever seen anything out there?"

"You mean like Old Twenny, the monster? No, but when the lads are out on the lake in their boat, inspecting and checking from time to time, they don't let their hands dangle in the water, either." Lancelot Yeo laughed.

"Twenny, the monster? Is there talk among your men of some sort of a monster out there?" I laughed, too.

"Oh good heavens, no. I'm sorry I mentioned it. I hope you're not going to bring that nonsense up in court."

"My goodness, no," I assured him. "You've given me everything I need in order to confirm that I made the right decision in advising my client he should back off. But during my inquiries, I've heard vague murmurings about something in the lake."

"Oh, you must have run into old Uncle Hughie Tucker. He's the main culprit."

"Yes, I've talked to him," I said. "He tells some good stories, all right. But he seems intent on debunking the whole idea of a monster in the lake."

"The tried and true technique of a master spinner of tall tales," said Lancelot Yeo. "Spread your blather around everywhere and say you don't believe a word of it, that it's all a lot of drivel—it gives credibility to you as the spreader of the nonsense to begin with. But he's not alone in his yarns out there."

"You've heard of others?"

"Well, you know, a lot of people around here come originally from Devon in England and Waterford in Ireland," said the Englishman. "Delightful counties, both of them, but both could be described as domains of moors, bogs, and monsters, not to mention fairies, fiends, ogres, giants, trolls, and gnomes. All highly transportable across the Atlantic, evidently, and all right at home out here in Newfoundland.

"It's the same with names of things. Take Devon and their ponds, for example. They have no body of water large enough there to constitute a lake, so they don't even use the term. Everything is a pond. When they came over here, therefore, all bodies of water, big or small, were ponds. Hence a body of water relatively larger than the rest and entitled to be designated a lake anywhere else but Devon and here, had to have a size designation stuck on the word *pond* to elevate it above the ordinary. Ergo, Twenty Mile Pond."

"It's a good name, though," I said. "I like it, personally."

"As do I, except for the fact that it gives the impression that the people who first saw it were so unworldly as to be flabbergasted by the huge size of that little lake just twenty miles in perimeter. Probably not even that big, since some say that the twenty miles is the distance from St. John's to the end of the lake and back to St. John's again. In fact, it's a pathetically small body of water, as anyone who tries, as I must, to keep a few gallons of H_2O in it during a dry August, is painfully aware."

"To your knowledge, has it ever gone dry or nearly dry?"

"No, no. A slight exaggeration there on my part. But the idea that it is capacious enough to contain a monstrosity of some sort is ludicrous. Yet some such notion seems to persist, even among those who ought to know better. There was another episode recently that briefly fanned the fire among a few gullible yokels.

"A helicopter pilot flying over Windsor Lake thought he saw a huge, grotesque shape moving under the water, but it disappeared as abruptly as it appeared. He was so intrigued that he flew lower and lower and landed on a spit of land out in the middle. There's even a video on social media of the chopper landing. But absolutely no one has reported a similar sighting before or since, either from a helicopter or a low-flying water bomber. The pilot himself said afterwards that it had to have been a trick of the light. And of course, as a lawyer interested in the nature of proof, yourself, you will appreciate that the inability to authenticate a sighting of something, or to duplicate an experiment, or to repeat an experience reported anecdotally, is the very definition of 'non-scientific.' I rest my case." Lancelot Yeo slapped the top of his desk with both hands rather decisively.

Needless to say, I didn't try out my sighting of a tentacle whipping out of the lake and seizing a gull in mid-air on him.

CHAPTER sixteen

On my next visit to Hughie Tucker, he said to me, "You'd better get as much out of me as fast as you can, because I'm getting married and moving into another suite with the new wife in a little while."

I passed him the flask of rum. "Congratulations. Where are you going to hide this then?"

"I won't need to. Love conquers all. I won't have to drown my sorrows nearly so much then. One a day from the front desk will be enough. The new wife likes her one ounce of rye a day, too, so we're all set for having our snort together. Right compatible."

"But why won't I be able to get any more out of you after you get married?"

"Too busy doing the husband-wife thing, b'y. She said the both of us will be 'prioritizing our activities' more then. That means picking and doing the stuff that she thinks is good and important."

"Good job I got here before that happens, Hughie. Because I was talking to a man the other day who says you're the main culprit when it comes to spreading around myths about Old Twenny. He swears you only pretend you don't believe the guff you're throwing out in order to give greater credibility to yourself as a source of the nonsense. I'm glad I got a chance to get your take on that."

"That arrogant Limey fella, right? I met a lot like him when I was overseas in the war. Some people find him very hard to take, but then we probably only won the war because the Brits thought they were so much superior to everyone else. How could they possibly lose, up against a bunch of Huns and wops? They were too good to lose, so they didn't lose. You've got to love their attitude."

"I'm not saying who it was, Hughie. That's not important. What's important is that it made me think you do, in fact, believe there's something out there."

"Whether I do or not, what you've got to ask yourself is this: If there is something out there, where in the name of God could it have possibly come from?"

"And?"

"There's an old guy down in Horse Cove who's got some ideas on that."

"Horse Cove? That's St. Thomas, down by Portugal Cove, right? Do you know what he says?"

"Yes, but you should get it from the horse's mouth. Tommy Squires. He claims he's a descendant of Tommy Picco from down that way."

"*The* Tommy Picco? The young fellow who saved everyone in

the boat by chopping off the huge tentacles of a giant squid that were wrapped around it, pulling them under?"

"One and the same, sir. You'd better see him quick, though, Bill. I haven't heard he died, but I don't know how much longer he's got for this world. Geez, when he goes and I go, there won't be anyone left to spread around the whoppers." Hughie picked up the phone. "I'll give him a shout and tell him you're coming. He doesn't reveal everything he knows to just anyone. Now what's his number? I haven't talked to him for six months." He dialled a number from memory. "And, Bill, don't mind what I said before: when I'm hitched you can still come and visit whenever you want. Just call first to see if I'm here. She's got me mesmerized with 'activities.' Next week we're going to the Arts and Culture Centre for something or other." He smiled happily. "Did you ever hear the like, the Arts and—? Oh. Uncle Tommy, how're you doing, it's Hughie. Good, good. Listen, I've got this big important lawyer here who's so clever he appreciates a drop of black rum, and he wants . . ."

CHAPTER seventeen

Driving to Uncle Tommy Squires's house, I passed the home of my old girlfriend's parents, or what used to be their house. Were they still there? She herself had moved to Vancouver years ago, generating another unholy row regarding the kids and their father. But the sight of the house brought on a feeling in me now, as it had not done any time I'd driven by it in the past twenty years, of ineffable sadness. I'd had some great times there with Ramona. Maybe my abrupt abandonment of her had brought out that nasty, mad side of her. Maybe if I had wed her, we would have had a marriage as marvellous as the two years that preceded my vision, and I wouldn't be afflicted now by this—face it—unresolvable and ceaseless anxiety over Molly and Esme.

I recognized as I passed the house the reasons behind my nostalgic sentiments: I was being faint-hearted in the face of this ghastly challenge presented by my two teenaged responsibilities, and that had spurred me into being egotistic enough to think that I, the wonderful and lovable me, could have altered a woman's basic character.

I dismissed all that and pulled into Tommy Squires's driveway. He lived in a neat little local-style saltbox house that, as Hughie Tucker had described it, looked like a beautiful rough pearl in a box of tinsel and spangles, in among those big, modern, glitzy abodes that had taken over the shore.

Hughie had told me that Tommy was well into his eighties and nearly blind, but acute of mind, and that his slightly younger sister, Melissa, lived with him. After our hellos she excused herself, "to let you men talk your important business," and went out of the parlour, grinning, into the kitchen.

Uncle Tommy started right in. He was a great-great—he didn't know how many greats—nephew of the famous Tommy Picco. In fact, he was named after him. He supposed that I knew all about what young Tommy had done way back in October of 1873.

I said I had a general knowledge of the adventure, and he said he'd better give me a brief summary, then, to make sure, before getting to the other stuff that was not well-known at all, hardly known by anyone, and he wouldn't be telling me now—no offence—if Hughie Tucker hadn't vouched for me.

He started his narrative, and proceeded as if he was reading from a script. He'd recited this before. Twelve-year-old Tommy Picco from Portugal Cove was out on Conception Bay in a dory that fall with a couple of fishermen. Suddenly, at a distance, they saw a big heap of something floating on the water. One of them thought it might be wreckage of some sort, but no one really had any idea what it was as they rowed over to it. When they got close enough, one of the men poked at it with a gaff.

Immediately, the massive heap came to life and loomed up out of the water. It was a huge, ugly monstrosity. It had enormous green eyes as big as dinner plates, which looked at the fishermen with a fury that terrified them. A big, hard, sharp beak protruded from the middle of its face, like a giant parrot's beak, and two of its thick, long arms, which had suckers with teeth on them, wrapped themselves around the boat and started to pull it over and under.

Young Tommy Picco moved fast. He grabbed a hand axe and chopped frantically at the tentacles that gripped the boat until he had severed them. All the while the wounds gushed blue blood, and the monster finally hurtled away under the water, spurting massive clouds of black ink. No one in the boat doubted that twelve-year-old Tommy had saved the lives of all on board.

Meanwhile, the severed tentacles flopped down in the boat and were brought to shore. The larger one was eaten by dogs; the fishermen kept the smaller one. When it was stretched to its full length, it turned out to be nearly nineteen feet long. The men awarded the tentacle to Tommy for his courage and quick thinking.

Tommy's clergyman in Portugal Cove told him of the Reverend Moses Harvey in St. John's, an eminent naturalist who had a worldwide reputation for examining strange creatures and monstrosities of the deep. He had made it known that he particularly wanted to obtain samples of the fearsome "devil fish," the giant squid, which Tommy's clergyman thought the tentacle might belong to.

Driven by a desire to advance scientific knowledge, though some have suggested he might also have had thoughts of a reward in mind, young Tommy brought the tentacle into the city by wagon and delivered it to Dr. Harvey. The renowned naturalist was overjoyed and recompensed Tommy most suitably.

Now, just in case anyone had become skeptical of the truth of Tommy Picco's exploit, Tommy Squires said to me, there was a historically documented case from Logy Bay just a month later. Fishermen there found a whole giant squid dead in their nets, and they carried it in to Moses Harvey as well. A picture at the university in St. John's showed the big squid draped over some sort of a crossbar, with its tentacles, many feet long, doubled over and hanging down into Dr. Harvey's bath.

Tommy's sister, Melissa, called out from the kitchen: "It's on the Internet, too. You can see it there plain as day. I can only imagine what his poor wife must've thought."

"So all of that is well-known," said Uncle Tommy Squires. "But what I'm going to tell you now, sir, is hardly known to the public at large at all. It's been a family secret for generations."

Melissa appeared in the doorway with a big grin on her face; I could tell she was trying not to laugh at her brother's words. "Would you two like a cup of tea?" she asked.

"Or something with a bit of a harder kick?" inquired Tommy, hopefully. I turned down both offers and urged him to go on.

The success of the Logy Bay fishermen with their whole squid caused intense competition, he said. That same autumn young Tommy Picco and some friends caught two smaller squids in nets in Conception Bay, two juveniles they thought might be giant squid youngsters—though, some said, they were more like octopuses—and put them still alive in a barrel of sea water. They loaded the barrel aboard their wagon to carry the creatures in to Professor Harvey. They drove by Twenty Mile Pond, right where the old Portugal Cove Road ran very close to the water, and there and then the squid, or whatever they were, started to flail about in the barrel most alarmingly. It was almost as if they could sense the closeness of the big pond even though it was fresh water.

The boys tried to keep the barrel upright and struggled to keep the lid on, but in the commotion, the barrel fell off the cart and the two creatures slithered out, slunk across the few feet of beach rocks, and dived right into the pond. The boys were frightened to death and swore not to say a word to anyone about this accident because, only shortly before, the pond had become the new water supply for the city. They knew that the squids would not live long in fresh water and they were worried that the dead bodies would soon be discovered floating on the surface. Of course, everyone in Portugal Cove knew what they'd been up to, so Tommy Picco and the others were sure to get the blame for befouling the drinking water reservoir, when the corpses surfaced.

They waited and waited, often going to Twenty Mile Pond to scan the waves and the shores for any signs, hoping that they could retrieve the bodies before anyone else saw them and skedaddle out of there. But no bodies ever appeared, and, save for some chosen family members of Tommy Picco's who knew the truth, nothing was heard of the unfortunate mishap ever again. Except, perhaps, that some busybodies started trying to frighten everyone by spreading around rumours about something scary in the lake.

"Can you remember any rumours, Mr. Squires?"

"Uncle Hughie Tucker is the best one for that part of it. He can give it to you chapter and verse."

"He certainly can," I said. "I've had some grand chats with him. Well, that was very interesting, Mr. Squires. I can't thank you enough for telling me all about Tommy Picco."

"Oh, my pleasure," smiled Uncle Tommy, "no thanks required. But speaking of Hughie Tucker, did I hear him right when he said you have impeccable taste in black rum?"

"Tommy, what next!" said his sister from the kitchen.

"You did hear right," I said, "and by coincidence, I happen to have a bottle right here in my briefcase just to prove my good taste."

"That's better than the Member of the House for this district. He came in looking for our votes one day a couple of years ago and he was sitting where you are now, that very chair, sir, when he opened this box he was carrying around—"

"Attaché case," said Melissa from the kitchen.

"Opened this attaché case, pretending to look for some

important documents. My eyesight was still good in those days, and I looked in. You know the only thing he was lugging around in his fancy attaché case? A ham sandwich, sir."

The three of us laughed, and I thanked the good Tommy and Melissa Squires again, accepted their open invitation to come back and have a Jiggs' dinner with them and sample the rum at the same time, and went out to resume my quest.

CHAPTER eighteen

Dr. Max Atwood, professor emeritus of marine biology at Memorial University, was a world-renowned expert on giant squid. I called him, introduced myself, and asked if I could make an appointment to meet with him.

He responded, "Yes, by all means. But may I inquire what our meeting might be in aid of?"

"The giant squid has come up in a case I'm handling, and, quite frankly, I've become fascinated with the creature and would like to gain some additional knowledge."

"Could this lead to my becoming an expert witness in Supreme Court?" asked the professor. "I've always wanted to do that. I've examined in my lab, by myself or with my predecessor, at least twenty giant squid over the years and I've even had a species of squid named after me. Supreme Court would be a good forum for spreading the ink about the giant squid—ink in the newspapers, you understand. Don't be alarmed: I shan't use that atrocious pun on the witness stand."

"That's an excellent pun, sir. And we can discuss how to use it to best advantage, because expert testimony before court about the giant squid is a distinct possibility. Which, by the way, is not something I ever expected to say when I first started my law practice."

"Alas, I know. It's no wonder the general public is still abysmally ignorant of the true character of these natural marvels."

"True, true. Twenty giant squid, you say, Professor Atwood? That's a lot of arms, or is it feet?"

Atwood giggled. "One of my students once said that the coast of Newfoundland is 'maggoty with the foot-headed friggers.' I myself wouldn't go that far, but we do appear to have more than our fair share of the giant squid variety of the head-footed wonders stranded around our coast at fairly regular, but long, intervals."

"About how often would that be?"

"Our esteemed Dr. Fred Aldrich," said the professor, "former head of this department, reckoned it to be every ninety years or so. He predicted the appearance on our shores of a plethora of giant squid in the late 1960s, some ninety years after the era of sightings that included our famous Tommy Picco's exploit with his particular devil fish in Conception Bay. I still have an office here at the university, by the way. Come up and we'll talk all about it and I'll show you around. We have an octopus specimen here, too."

"Are squid and octopi closely related?" I asked.

"You're lucky I'm not like my old mentor in New Zealand," he replied. "When I referred to octopi once, he said that the use of octopi as a plural bespeaks a distressingly vulgar ignorance of the classical languages. Octopodes would be the correct word for more than one octopus, he said. But rather than being pedantic, he suggested that we speak English and use the word *octopuses*. Octopuses. Good lord, I'd rather say octopi, but he ruined that word for me forever. So octopuses it shall be. Now, are squid and octopuses related, you ask? Very much so. Both of them are saltwater creatures called cephalopods because their feet come out of their heads, and they both have blue blood and three hearts and eight sucker-lined arms. Squids have two tentacles as well, with hooks on them, which they use to reach out and capture prey. There are at least three hundred species of each, which differ from one another in many physical ways and in how and where they live.

"Octopuses can be more than five metres in size and giant squid can be thirteen metres, or forty-three feet long for females, who are larger than the males, with unconfirmed reports of some measuring up to twenty metres, or sixty feet. Giant squid could very well be as long as a sperm whale.

"Octopuses can live up to three years, and squid up to five. But, and this is interesting, there can be a convergence between squid and octopuses as well. For example, there's one highly successful squid called the vampire squid that combines features of octopuses and squids in a unique, one-off, evolutionary formula. Am I going too fast? Of course, on the witness stand, I would be much slower and more deliberate."

"No, no," I said. "This is fascinating. Did I read somewhere that some squid are like chameleons and can change colour?"

"Yes, in a squid, the skin is covered in pigment-containing cells, chromatophores, which allow the squid to instantly match its colour to its environment. Some octopuses are reported to have this, too."

I remembered Lancelot Yeo's mention of the pilot. "So, if you were looking down at a giant squid, or a large octopus containing those cells, from a helicopter that was flying low over the water, and the squid or octopus vanished suddenly, that ability it has to change its colour could be the cause of its disappearance?"

"Oh, absolutely. And octopuses and squids can move very fast as well, by jet propulsion, expelling water out of a siphon. Both can swim in every direction, and change course instantly. And, in case you were afraid to ask, yes, there is lovemaking among our head-footed friends, too. Males of both groups fertilize the eggs of the females in various ways. The mind boggles at the permutations and combinations involved with all those tentacles, so I won't go into detail for fear of arousing jealousy. Ha ha ha."

"Ha ha ha," I went, joining in the hilarity. "I saw a TV documentary a while back about the tremendous intelligence of octopuses. Is that your experience with giant squid, too?"

"These are great questions. I'm looking forward to Supreme Court. But, Mr. McGill, come up, come up."

CHAPTER nineteen

In the lab at the university, Professor Atwood showed me specimens and pictures of squid and octopuses. As we moved about, he picked up where we'd left off on the phone the day before.

"Are they intelligent? Oh yes. Oh yes. Squid and octopuses are the most intelligent of the invertebrates and are an important example of the evolution of intelligence in animals. Research has concluded that octopuses can learn by observing, and possess exceptional ability regarding spatial learning, navigation, and hunting techniques.

"It has been difficult to study the intelligence of live giant squid in controlled circumstances, but from dead specimens it is clear that the giant squid has a sophisticated nervous system and complex brain. And if the Humboldt squid, the aggressive 'red devil,' a smaller but still large cousin of the giant squid, is anything to go by, their hunting forays in packs for schools of fish show remarkable co-operation and communication and indicate they are very likely as intelligent as the octopus.

"The requirement of giant squid to locate and capture their prey in the vast, deep ocean and to evade sperm whales, probably their only predator judging by the beaks found inside these whales' stomachs, has been a driving force behind the development of their advanced intelligence and those eyes. Giant squid, and their cousin, the colossal squid, have the largest eyes of any creature alive. The record for the diameter of a pair of eyes measured to date is twenty-seven centimetres, or nearly a foot wide."

"This is intriguing, Professor Atwood. If the giant squid is as intelligent as the octopus, that's really saying something. Because in that documentary I saw, the octopuses had the ability to use tools. They salvaged coconut shells thrown out by humans, and carried them off and assembled them into a shelter. They even picked up and transported tools, and saved them to use later in the building of complex dens and fortresses. They were able to learn how to escape from convoluted mazes simply by watching another octopus that had been trained to escape. They could even open the screw caps on containers."

"Yes, yes," said the professor. "Yes, yes. Both octopuses and squid have a high level of dexterity, and the same ability necessary for tool use and manipulation that we humans have. The highly sensitive suction cups and prehensile arms of octopuses and squid are just as good at holding and handling objects as the human hand."

"Didn't I read somewhere about an octopus at an aquarium in Germany who could juggle?"

"Oh yes, that would be dear Otto," answered Atwood. "There are reports of Otto the octopus juggling the hermit crabs in his tank, and often, he will decide to redecorate his tank, and then he will proceed to rearrange everything in there to suit his taste. Sometimes, for mischief, he deliberately takes aim and throws rocks at the aquarium glass, smashing it."

"He actually breaks the glass? That's a lot of force. Their arms or tentacles must be very strong?"

"Well, they are all muscle."

Now I came to our case: "Would a giant squid be strong enough to throw a man a few feet through the air, ten or twelve feet, for example, do you think?"

"I've never heard of such a thing happening in nature," replied the professor. "They may weigh hundreds of kilograms, but they really are gentle giants. So, unless you're prepared to volunteer to provoke one into doing it to you in the lab, ha ha. . . . On principle, I'd have to say yes, though—easily strong enough.

"Now, just to finish with Otto the octopus," he went on, "he has caused short-circuits for fun in the lighting system in the aquarium by crawling out of his tank and shooting a jet of water at the overhead light."

"Amazing. Otto sounds like an exceptional genius among octopuses. Do you think a giant squid could be that smart?"

"Well, here's an example of squid intelligence," he said, "in the form of communication that has been observed to take place between some social species of squid. They use control of their skin colour and their ability to rapidly change that colour, which evolved originally as camouflage, to communicate, apparently meaningfully, with one another in courtship and mating rituals. Members of one species of squid in the Caribbean can even send a particular message, by changing and flashing skin colours and patterns, to a squid on their right, while they send another, different message to a squid on their left."

"They must have a pretty sizable brain," I said. "Is that big bulbous head all brain?"

"Squid and octopuses have a very high brain-to-body mass ratio, by far the highest of all invertebrates. And our giant squid possesses huge nerve cells that are the largest found in any animal alive, and which control escape and attack behaviours. A single nerve cell can be thirty centimetres long.

"The very instant the squid's brain says 'Escape!' or 'Attack!' she's off. There is absolutely no delay in transmitting the 'go' message between synapses as there is in other animals; for instance, something slow, say, like a cheetah. Ha ha. So, all considered, whether a giant squid can be as smart as Otto the octopus is still a challenging question, but I would say they are certainly in the same ballpark of intelligence."

"When I was googling the giant squid a while ago," I said, "I came across a philosopher in the UK who said he saw clear evidence in a video of a giant squid that it demonstrated true feelings, which others, I think, have taken as an indication that it possessed consciousness."

"Yes, that would be the philosopher, Professor David Cockburn, at the University of Wales, where he lectures on the philosophy of mind. He saw a video of a giant squid that must have thought it was under attack by the photographer with the video camera, and the squid showed unmistakable signs of being afraid. It cringed and trembled and winced. What was amazing about it to Cockburn was that you could clearly see in the reaction of the squid, so different in appearance from a human being, the unambiguous emotion of fear which one human being would readily recognize in another. Clearly, the giant squid possessed a high level of consciousness."

"It would be interesting to capture one alive and do some brain scans to see what is going on in there."

"Let me know when you catch one alive and kicking," he said. "So far, regrettably, any giant squid captured alive has either died in the process or very soon afterwards."

I came to the crux of my inquiry: "Do any octopuses or squid live in lakes or rivers?"

"Some anecdotes have come to us of octopuses and squid having been seen in bodies or streams of fresh water. There are no confirmed cases, though. I suppose it's not absolutely impossible, but nothing has been proved, and I would have to judge it as highly improbable. It's all a matter of osmosis. They never developed a sodium pump that would help them cope with the demands of osmosis in fresh water. I would have to conclude, really, that there's no way a giant squid or octopus could survive in fresh water at all, and certainly not for a long period of time."

"What about salmon, though, or sea trout, or eels, Dr. Atwood? Salmon are born and develop in fresh water, then migrate downstream to spend their adult lives in salt water, and end up coming back to fresh water to spawn."

"Yes, to spawn and to die, usually. The attempt to change back to fresh water and the trauma of it seems to be what kills them. Salmon and the others have evolved over hundreds of thousands of years to make those adaptations to fresh water, and to brackish water at the mouth of the stream, and then salt water, and back to brackish and fresh again. But no species of squid or octopus is reported to have evolved in that way."

"What about a sudden, spontaneous mutation," I offered, "that allowed a giant squid or octopus to survive if it happened to blunder into a river or lake?"

Professor Atwood smiled indulgently. "A glance at some of the ocean species and their behaviours would convince the most skeptical marine biologist that nothing seems impossible out there in the briny deep, in evolutionary terms. For instance, I mentioned the vampire squid, which combines features of octopuses and squids in a unique evolutionary formula that has survived for millions of years. It lives hundreds of metres down and feeds exclusively on the decaying dead descending through the water. It occupies a classification category all of its own, the only species in its order, *Vampyroteuthis infernalis*. The 'squid from hell.'

"But I would have to say that the possible mutation you just described would be an extremely naive view of the way evolutionary change by way of genetic mutations works. There is no way that such a non-incremental, sudden mutation could have taken place to develop sophisticated survival machinery back and forth between salt and fresh water, or, better said, the odds are astronomically against it."

"But, Dr. Atwood, what if I were to tell you that over a hundred years ago, young Tommy Picco allowed two squid-like creatures to escape into Windsor Lake and that they were never seen again, even floating dead on the water? And that there have been reports of some sort of large creature in the lake ever since."

"Mr. McGill, I live on St. Thomas Line, not far from there, and I recall reading in a history of the area about a battle royal that took place around the time of Tommy Picco between residents there and St. John's city officials over making the lake the main water supply for the city. Just like the battle of Foxtrap, when residents protested the railway going through.

"People in the vicinity of Twenty Mile Pond were outraged that they wouldn't be able to fish there anymore, or hunt or snare rabbits, or boat there, or build cabins, or have skating parties, or do anything else in or around the lake for recreation, as they had been doing for generations. I'm not surprised that scary stories were invented by both sides to either drive the water-supply people away and make them drop the project, on the one hand, or to stop the livyers there from continuing their previous activities on the lake, on the other."

I decided to try out my experience on him. "Okay, then, but don't think me mad altogether when I tell you that over twenty years ago I saw from Portugal Cove Road, cold sober late one summer afternoon, an osprey stop suddenly above the water in its dive and fly off again fast, and, at the same instant, a thick tentacle emerge from Windsor Lake and snatch a seagull right out of the air."

"I don't think you mad, my good man," said Atwood. "Not in the least. I'm a bit of a photography buff and a film freak, and I have often discussed with a friend from Quebec, who is a filmmaker, the pictures and film we've taken here in Newfoundland. We both agreed that on some days there is nothing in the world as extraordinary as the air and the light in this province for filming. I'm guessing now, but I'd say that on the day in question the sky was cloudless, the sun you were looking into was low and bright, blinding even, and the wind was from a northerly direction, making the air as clear as crystal."

"Very much like that, Professor, yes."

"I imagined as much, and I say that because I was filming from a longliner in Bonavista Bay on a day like that, trying to confirm reported sightings of a giant squid. All of a sudden I saw a killer whale, an orca, rise right out of the water for a split second, seize a seal in its mouth from the surface, and instantly disappear again.

"I say I saw it, but nobody else on board did. And I never saw the orca or any sign of seals afterwards. Nor did anyone else on board or on shore. What is more, I'd been filming precisely where I'd been looking when I saw the phenomenon, but there was nothing whatsoever of that nature on the developed film. So, what can one say? It was as if my mind took advantage of the conditions— weather, atmosphere, water, low blinding sun. Deciding they were ideal for something dramatic to happen, it supplied the missing drama of its own volition. Probably as a result of my watching too many nature shows on TV. So, what would be your lawyer's rejoinder to that, Mr. McGill?"

"We lawyers do recognize, Dr. Atwood, that first-hand, so-called eyewitness accounts can be very imprecise, dubious, and unreliable. But on the other hand, that's no reason to dismiss them entirely, simply because the event seen was improbable. The reasons you gave to explain away your vision of the killer whale and the seal are certainly thought-provoking, but frankly, the explanation may be just as dubious and fanciful as the existence of your sighting itself. Moreover, I'd require some additional evidence that your camera continued, in fact, to point directly at the phenomenon itself, which must have startled and astonished you when it first came into your line of vision."

I saw the professor stiffen and bristle in annoyance at what he must have considered a dilettante upstart's challenge to his professorial authority, but he remained silent. I went on. I described to him the cases: the governor's granddaughter being helped ashore by some huge creature when by all accounts she should have drowned; the Multi-Million Dollar Man, about to desecrate the shoreline and being grabbed by something in the lake and never seen or heard from again; a client of my firm, a young lady accused of murder, who insisted that the victim was flung up against a tree at a height of eight feet and killed. "How would you respond to assertions, Professor, that there is something—call it a monster—in the lake?"

Atwood studied me with some hauteur for ten seconds before speaking. "I trust, sir, that you are not considering calling me as an expert witness in the hope of confirming the legitimacy of those anecdotes. My professional services are available solely in support of science, and naught else. To any lawyer as would query me about such tales on a witness stand in court, I must needs respond to in this manner: you may, if you wish, practise your sophist's art of making the worse argument seem the better by multiplying together such baseless and unfounded incidents, that is to say, you may continue to practise law, and I, if I may, shall confine myself to proven facts derived from the science of marine biology."

Call me defeatist, but I deemed further interrogation of Professor Atwood futile.

CHAPTER twenty

The winter that crept upon us, nearly unnoticed while we fretted about the case, settled in as an unusually frigid, relatively windless one, with very little snow. Ponds and lakes were well frozen over by early January, and the delight of the city's children and adults all month was to go skating and to play outdoor hockey on the natural rinks found everywhere.

All the bodies of water I passed in the city one weekend—Quidi Vidi, Kent's Pond, Kenny's Pond, Burton's Pond, Virginia Waters, Long Pond, Mundy Pond—were like nostalgia scenes from the cover of a *New Yorker* magazine: hundreds of young and grown-up bodies twirled or glissaded or raced across the ice, and makeshift hockey goals sprang up in the middle of it all. On a whim, I drove out Portugal Cove Road until I reached Twenty Mile Pond, which I hadn't looked at since the freezing set in.

The contrast with the other ponds and lakes was striking. The ice on the surface was nearly clear of snow and visible everywhere, with the occasional swirl kicked up now and then by a light gust of wind. But the lake was entirely empty. There wasn't a soul on the large expanse of ice.

A bright idea worthy of our Esme came into my mind: after dark I should go out on the ice and see if I could spot anything moving in the water below. A monster, say. Yes, Esme would probably take it into her head to do just that. She and I must share the same gene for "adventure."

That night, I told Jennifer I was going to the office for a couple of hours, but when I was about to get in my car, I went and opened the trunk instead, and looked in. There in a corner were the crampons I sometimes pulled over the soles of my boots for traction on road ice during winter walks. With their presence confirmed, the temptation became too great. I drove out to Twenty Mile Pond and parked my car beside it.

A flashlight and camera phone stowed in my outer pockets, I put on the crampons and crept a few feet out on the ice. Many Newfoundlanders called the crampons "creepers." A good descriptive name for them tonight. I hoped the ice was safe. Other natural ice surfaces on ponds had been measured and found to be at least five inches thick, sturdy enough to hold people, snowmobiles, and all-terrain vehicles. But of course this lake's ice had not been measured for safety; nobody was supposed to be on it. I could only take it on faith that the springs that fed the lake were all cold, none warm. Edging my way out in the dark and concentrating as best I could on the condition of the ice, I heard constant sounds of groaning and loud cracking travelling across the lake. The night was overcast, with some blowing snow, so I thought I wouldn't be very visible from the road. The black expanse of nothingness, the bitter temperature, the sudden, hostile squalls of wind—I felt so alone and lost, the sensation was physically painful. If I were to perceive something monstrous under the ice, I didn't know if I would die of shock or welcome it as a friend.

But apparently I wasn't as alone and invisible and lost as I felt. There was a shout behind me. I turned and saw two cars stopped near mine; one of them was now shining its headlights on high beam right at me.

A man called out: Was everything all right? I replied in the affirmative and crept back toward the shore, thinking that one of the glories of Newfoundland and Labrador was that everyone tried to look out for everyone else. But tonight the only thing this laudable tradition accomplished was to ruin my damned monster patrol.

Back on shore, I told them my sweater had blown out there and I was trying to retrieve it, but it looked like I'd lost it forever. They listened to me and then glanced at each other as if to say that my sweater might not be the only thing I'd lost forever. Then one of them asked, "Aren't you Mr. McGill? We met at a reception last year. My wife works in the same building as your wife."

The next evening at dinner, Jennifer asked me what I thought I'd been doing out in the middle of Windsor Lake the previous night, creeping about all by myself in the dark. Her neighbour in the office building had been accurately briefed by her husband.

I shook my head and laughed a little. "I told you, I was heading for the office. The scenic route."

"Did you ever find your ghost sweater?"

"I may have been mistaken about that. It may still be in the closet."

"How about your ghost monster? Any sightings?"

"No, he's still in the closet, too. I'm sorry, Jennifer, I was taken by a whim, and it was such a nice night for it. I should have told you, but I was trying to keep my lunacy from you a little while longer, if I could."

"I don't know if it's lunacy, Bill, but you do seem to be a bit obsessive about that lake and whatever you imagine is in it."

"Grasping at straws is what I'm doing." A sigh burst out of me. "God, those poor silly little girls."

Jennifer got up and came around the table. She enfolded my head in her arms and kissed me. "I know," she whispered, and kissed me again. "I know."

Molly suddenly materialized in the kitchen. Then I heard Matthew bouncing down over the stairs. They'd been late getting home because, after her diving practice, Molly had had to pick up her brother from his rehearsal for the class play: he was playing Nagg, the man in the garbage can in *Endgame*. She glanced at us now, feigning indifference as Jennifer withdrew her arms from me, although she did say, "Not hard to know it's only two weeks till Valentine's Day." She opened the oven door. "Ah, lasagna. Lamb, is it?"

"Nothing but your favourites around these parts, Your Highness."

"My favourite is chicken," said Matthew from the doorway.

"Yeah, but you're only the boy," said Molly.

"I really miss Esme around here. When is Aunt Maggie going in for therapy again?"

"Chicken next time," said Jennifer.

Matthew went to the notepad by the phone, wrote on a piece of paper, tore it off, and stuck it on the fridge door under a magnet. "Note to self for English: Good definition of 'forlorn hope'— chicken next time."

Molly had to smile, and Jennifer laughed. "Poor child. Promise me you'll hide that when child welfare raids the place. How's Nagg coming along?"

"Great, I think. The drama coach says I take to a garbage can like a duck takes to water."

"He's famous," said Molly, "for spotting talent."

As they bantered, it crossed my mind that I hadn't heard Molly coming down the stairs or walking through the hall before she strolled into the kitchen. I wondered if she'd been out there eavesdropping on the conversation between Jennifer and me. If she hadn't been, then the way she and Esme duplicated my dangerous folly a few days later was a pretty huge coincidence.

CHAPTER twenty-one

Jennifer had to drive to Clarenville for the weekend to visit her mother and father, who were both down with the flu. If she'd been home, she would have heard Molly sneaking out of the house at two-thirty Saturday morning. I never asked Matthew if he'd heard her, or had known what she was planning, because I didn't want to force him, ever, into a future choice of having either to lie to me or to rat out his sister.

As for myself, after a rough, nearly sleepless week dealing with the legal consequences of a safety crisis on a helicopter ferrying workers to an offshore oil rig, I was semi-comatose all Friday evening in front of the TV set and then zonked out all night in my bed. So, fortunately, nobody stopped Molly and Esme and their friends.

The next evening, Molly invited Esme and two boys they knew to our house for pizza. She asked Matthew and me to join them. The boys, Craig and Dwayne, had been a year ahead of Esme and Molly at school and were now in their first year at Memorial University. Esme was equally friendly with both, just buddies apparently, but extra chemistry was obvious between Molly and Craig.

He was tall and good-looking, heading for medical school, or so he hoped, and big in sports, especially volleyball. I realized this must have been the lad Jennifer had mentioned to me during the past fall, who had caused Molly to shriek in ecstasy over the phone to Esme because he had invited her to the Halloween dance at Memorial.

The other boy, Dwayne, apparently just a sidekick, jumped into our conversation around the kitchen table, saying, apropos of nothing, that he lived with his mother in St. John's, but on visits to his father in Blaketown, they often went ice fishing on Dildo Pond. Molly and Esme looked at him in satisfaction for his contribution, for some reason.

"What an interesting name for a pond," said Esme. "I wonder what else people do around there besides fishing?" She and Molly and the three boys laughed. I did, too, but less genuinely. And I shot the girls a bit of a look. The last thing I wanted Molly to do was to give an impression of fake-sophisticated looseness to Craig, her teenaged Romeo. He seemed a little too self-confident, a bit too full of himself, to suit me.

Molly caught my look and said, "You can relax, Dad. Aside from the odd murder every now and then, we're not totally degenerate yet."

They all cackled at that, accompanied by head shaking at the

126

absurdities that life imposed. Dwayne said, "My father thinks that Dildo is from Italian for delight, *diletto*. It's just as harmless, he says, as the name Heart's Delight is, farther out Trinity Bay."

"Italian?" said Craig. "If he believes that, tell him I'm an agent for an honest Italian broker named Ponzi who's got some great investments for sale." They all laughed again, Molly most of all. She was right in love with this guy.

After the pizza feast, Molly said they were going to play Scrabble. Who else wanted in? Matthew uttered the word *Scrabble* with a terrified look on his face and responded that, tragically, he'd already told his buddy he was going over to his house to watch the hockey game. Even to my antiquated way of thinking, Scrabble seemed to be an unusually conservative way for seventeen- and eighteen-year-olds of the opposite sex to be spending Saturday night.

I told them there were a few things I had to do, too, and went to my den. The only thing that rang true to me about their get-together was when I heard them out there whispering at length, keeping from me in my geezer's den the contents, no doubt naughty, of their plotting. Then Molly appeared in the den doorway. "Dad, have you got a minute to talk to us out in the kitchen?"

"I certainly do, sweetheart." I put down my file and went out.

"Now don't get mad," she said, as I sat down at the table.

"I'm not mad . . . yet." I forced a smile. God alone knew what was coming. One quarter to one half of the foursome pregnant? More criminal activities? "But you do have me frightened out of my wits."

"Dad, the four of us snuck out last night—early this morning, rather—and drove out to Windsor Lake." Then she and the others unfolded their story. They had slipped out of their respective homes and residences at 2:30 a.m., and Esme had picked the other three up. They arrived at Windsor Lake about three in the morning. They had selected that hour because vehicles would be scarce on the road. And they had consciously chosen last night because the forecast weather conditions seemed ideal. The moon was full and thick clouds were scudding past it so that, one minute, hardly anything was visible in the dark, and the next minute everything was brightly lit. All in all, with the dark intervals and the slight wind blowing some snow around, and the lack of traffic, they figured there was little risk of being seen.

Dwayne, the Dildo Pond ice fisher, had an auger with him which he always used to test the thickness of ice on ponds. His expertise in this area, known to Craig, was the reason he'd been asked along on the adventure. He found that the ice on Windsor Lake was seven inches thick a few feet from shore, which was sufficient even for a car to drive on safely. I had to admire to myself the intelligent preparedness they had displayed, but I could hardly bear the cocky adolescent confidence with which they now described it.

"That lake is spring-fed," I growled. "There might well have been dangerous, thin places anywhere."

Molly looked at me in surprise. "Dad, we're not idiots," she said. "Dwayne knew what he was doing, and we also had a couple of lengths of board and some rope with us for safety in case any of us suddenly broke through the ice. You were out there the other night all by yourself with no precautions or security measures at all—nothing. And you didn't even tell anyone you were doing it so we'd know where to go to look for the body."

"Yeah, but I'm an adult," I muttered. "I'm allowed to act stupid on my own. You're still minors in my care and so you have to ask for my mature consent to act stupid."

"If they're going to try us as adults," said Molly, "we're going to act like stupid adults when we feel like it."

Esme looked down from Molly's face with a smile. She always seemed to appreciate her cousin's comebacks.

"Point made," I murmured. "Go on."

"I didn't mean to be rude, Dad. But just wait till you hear what we saw."

They'd had flashlights but they didn't use them. They inched along in the dark when the moon was covered and lay down flat to hide from any observers when the moon shone bright. A few hundred feet out, when they were all lying on their bellies on the ice, Esme saw, directly below her eyes under the clear, transparent ice, something that looked like a big dinner plate.

She raised her head to get a better bead on the circular object, and she figured it measured about a foot in diameter. Nothing else was visible around it except black water. In the moonlight it looked green, with an inner black circle several inches wide. As she studied it, the circle startled her by moving. Suddenly it came to her: it was an eye, a huge green eye containing a large pupil, and it was staring right at her.

She got slowly to her knees, shushed the others, and motioned them toward her. She leaned back as Craig approached with his cellphone, bent right over the object, and took a picture. The flash went off, and they all saw the disc beneath the ice jerk away and then vanish. They heard creaking and groaning from the ice, and everybody had the feeling that it heaved upwards slightly, as if it was expanding or contracting from a temperature change. They all clamoured to look at the picture. There it was. They couldn't believe it. Craig had been able to capture the eye in his camera.

Craig pulled out his cellphone and showed me the image. As I examined it, I asked if they had other copies stored elsewhere. Yes, Craig said, he'd saved it in his computer, and he'd sent email attachments to the other three.

Their interpretation of the photo was more positive than mine, perhaps because they had actually seen the thing itself under the ice. For myself, I had to confess that the picture looked indefinite and ambiguous. If you weren't told what it was supposed to be, you could only say, really, that there was something round under the ice.

Craig had also taken a couple of distance shots of Dwayne and the two girls, three points of a triangle looking down at the ice between them. This was intended to show context and background for the object. But nothing was clearly visible under the ice in those pictures. In the close-up picture of the "eye," no context or background had been captured around the object. It might have been a hubcap, or a Frisbee, or a reflection of the moon off the ice coloured by some effect from the water beneath. Or it might have been a gigantic eye.

I told them the snaps were certainly intriguing, and

congratulated them on their initiative, but I kept my major misgivings to myself. I asked Craig to send copies of the shots to my email address because I was going to have them examined by an expert in marine biology at the university.

"Professor Atwood?" asked Craig. "He's retired but he still comes to the biology department all the time. He's world-famous. He'll know what it is."

The next day, when I found the girls by themselves watching a women's curling game on television, I said that, seriously, if they were ever thinking about doing anything so potentially dangerous again, to please at least discuss it with me first, and get my input. "Believe me," I said, "no one is more eager to find something in or around that lake to explain things than I am."

"*YesbutDad*," said Molly, "Esme is the one with a gun held to her head. She's got to act whenever she needs to. And she intends to, and she's right to." Molly spoke more forcefully than Esme would have. Esme remained silent, but her determined face indicated she agreed completely.

A realization came over me as I looked at them. All fall, and so far this winter, our lawyers had been treading water, focussed on legal procedures, and I'd been beavering away to come up with a few flimsy myths. But now, honestly and frankly, I was fully prepared to do anything at all—I mightn't yet know exactly what, but anything, whatever it took—to drag Esme and Molly out of this quagmire.

CHAPTER twenty-two

First thing Monday morning I sent an email to Professor Atwood, with the photo attachments, asking him to let me know what he thought the close-up might be an image of. He didn't email me back that day; I called him the next day and reached him. He talked to me as if I was a student pest badgering him to upgrade my marks to a pass.

"I was going to get back to you in due course," he said, "but, frankly, I had other, less frivolous, items on my agenda to attend to first. You ask what the object in the picture might be. Let me hazard a shrewd guess, which jumps out at me as a result of our earlier conversation. It looks vaguely like, or has been made to look like, the eye of a giant squid. But the representation is exceedingly unconvincing. It could be a snapshot of something else entirely and Photoshopped to look like a gargantuan eye. It's just sitting there as a distorted image with no setting or context to explicate it, or elucidate it, or size it, or locate it.

"The shots of the people kneeling on the ice don't necessarily even relate to it at all. And if, in fact, it is the eye of a large cephalopod, the likeness could easily have been stolen directly off the Internet. Give me an hour and I could probably find the very same picture on some website. There's a lot of research on giant squid these days, and a surfeit of pictures of giant squid and colossal squid, and their parts, including, naturally, their fascinating big eyes."

"I understand you perfectly, Professor Atwood," I said, "and I had similar doubts myself. However, four intelligent young witnesses are willing to testify to what they observed, and where and when they observed it, and that the photograph was taken of it at the time."

"And bright adolescent students have never been known to conspire to concoct an elaborate spoof for the fun of it? Or for the attention? That first-year student, Abbott, who allegedly took the picture—" It took me a moment to comprehend that he was talking about Craig, who had obviously approached him about this already. "—is under investigation for suspected plagiarism from Wikipedia for a term paper. And, B-T-W, as he might say, are any of our young photographic geniuses caught up in that dreadful drug and murder case, which originated by that very same lake? If so, it might well have been advantageous for them to fabricate a self-serving scenario designed to help extricate themselves."

I didn't say what I was thinking: everyone, even a lawyer-hater, is a damned attorney in a TV courtroom drama these days—they should ban all those productions from the screen before they metastasized even more into real life. I thanked the professor for his candid reaction and hung up the phone. In fact, he was more helpful than he might have believed.

His forceful denial that the pictures were scientific proof of anything set my mind on a different, murkier route. If I were to present them, together with the other dramatic "information" in my arsenal, on television and radio and the Internet and in newspapers, there could be just enough in the whole lot to cause questions and speculation in minds of many people watching, listening, and reading. It was a desperate, wicked stratagem: my sensational revelations at a news conference might, with luck, sow sufficient doubt in the minds of a potential jury chosen from such an audience.

Our lawyers had the snapshot of the big eye examined by a photographic expert. He pronounced the picture genuine and not Photoshopped. He would be prepared to state that much, but in no way could he assert confidently what the image in the snapshot might be. I would have to proclaim that myself with the rest, and perhaps be obliged to take on a discrediting attack by an authority like Dr. Atwood.

CHAPTER twenty-three

The prosecutor continued to try to set down Esme's preliminary inquiry for the spring. Morley Sheppard was surprised that the Crown seemed to be in an unholy rush. Murder charges in Canada usually proceeded to inquiry and trial slowly, and the prosecution seldom objected to requests for numerous delays by the defence to prepare their case. But in Esme's case, Derek Smythe was insisting on moving ahead with what looked like undue haste. He was babbling on, Morley said, about how a murder trial had to be treated as an urgent, top priority in the court system, and that justice delayed was justice denied for the Crown as well as the accused. Moreover, he was declaring this case so open-and-shut that no further delay was necessary. What could the defence possibly hope to come up with?

Morley confided to me that he was somewhat conflicted about whether to consent to the spring inquiry and move "this torment" along to trial, where we would get rid of the sword of Damocles over Esme's head one way or the other by a verdict, or continue to push for a delay to next fall in the desolate hope that something might turn up. There was no doubt in his mind that she would be bound over for trial at the inquiry. Oh yes, he could muddy the waters throughout on cross-examination and argument, but so far their only defence was, "Ladies and gentlemen of the jury, the prosecution has not proved the murder charge against Ms. Esme Browning by credible evidence beyond a reasonable doubt." He could hear the jurors, well aware of the drug-dealing circumstances, reacting to that in the jury room: "Yeah, right."

Our lawyers hid their anxiety from Esme and Molly during meetings with them. But to me, they suggested that Esme might want to consider a plea bargain, perhaps a guilty plea to manslaughter. In return, the Crown would have to agree to drop the motion to have them tried as adults, which would keep the girls' names from becoming public in the media, and allow for a greatly reduced sentence.

But Morley was not confident about any of it. He was painfully familiar with the bluster of prosecutors and he could generally tell when they were bluffing; unfortunately, they were giving every impression of believing their case to be rock solid. Really, all the Crown had to do, they were constantly saying, was plant these two rhetorical questions firmly in the jurors' minds about who and what had killed Jason Power: If not Esme Browning, the only person who was down there all alone with the victim, then who? And if not Esme's hiking pole, with the victim's blood on its sharp point, then what?

Just yesterday, Derek Smythe had said to Morley that the defence was in effect trying to argue that the Crown had to prove the victim was *not* speared in the eye by a branch more than two feet above his head, instead of the defence having to demonstrate clearly that such an inexplicable event was what in fact had happened. Did Morley actually believe the judge was going to let him get away with that? And if Morley somehow slipped that argument in by the back door, did he think it would cut any ice with a jury deliberating on a violent murder in a blatant drug trafficking case? What did the defence think the judge and jurors were, complete imbeciles?

"Bill, let me put it this way," said Morley Sheppard. "If I'm ever retained by the Crown to prosecute a murder case, I hope it's as strong for the prosecution as this one."

I hid my disgust from Morley over his rational judgments and solid good sense. I told him and Brian that I'd had a bright idea. Perhaps it might have the effect of provoking a fit of guffaws in the Department of Justice. Or maybe, just maybe, it might have the effect of getting the Crown to reconsider the charges altogether. I wanted Morley to arrange a meeting for me with Smythe, the Crown prosecutor, so that I could inform him, as a professional courtesy, of this unorthodox, even outrageous action, I proposed to take.

I intended to hold a news conference, as a parent of one of the accused girls and guardian of the other, to report publicly everything I knew, or had heard in my investigation, about the lake and its sinister inhabitant. That would include a description of my own sighting over twenty years ago; the oral and written reports of the experience on the lake of the governor and his granddaughter; the mysterious banning of fishing by governors thereafter; the stories from people in the vicinity of the lake, including that of the total disappearance of the Multi-Million Dollar Man and the strange sound his companions had heard at the lake at the time he vanished; the undoubted connection between the death of Jason Power, the drug trafficker, and something powerful and menacing in this body of water, including what Esme heard and saw at the time—the squawk and the trafficker's body flying by behind her; the unexplained blood and brain of the victim on a broken branch eight feet above the ground; and now the photograph of a monstrous eye beneath the ice.

I told Morley and Brian that they should disassociate themselves from what I was proposing to do, and state to the prosecutor that I was acting against their advice and without their consent.

"I certainly would have no problem," said Morley, "in advising you not to take that step and in stating that I do not consent to it. It would be an exceedingly irresponsible action for you to take as a parent and a guardian, and doubly so as a lawyer. You'd be inviting a citation for contempt of court, and worse, perhaps obstruction of justice charges. But more important than all that would be the possible unintended and unforeseen consequences to my clients. I have no idea how it might muddy the waters and undermine our defence. Think of the public's reaction, of incredulity, their serious doubts about our mental stability, which could play right into the hands of the prosecution. Remember that a jury has to be chosen from that same public."

"I think it is more likely that my disclosures would sow doubts about the charges against the girls in the minds of the general public, from which the jury will be picked."

"If that turns out to be so, then it could only be because it will bring about consternation, anxiety, even a wide-ranging alarm, about the danger to the public from the drinking water and from the lake in general. A lawyer might wish to ask himself if he wants to be accused, by doing this, of significant public mischief, possibly criminal in nature."

"Morley, listen, those possible consequences to me are trivial compared to any possible benefit to the girls."

"Harm to everyone would be the more likely outcome. Well, you are on your own on that. I'll be writing you a letter stating that I advised strenuously against it. And I'll have to inform Esme and Molly, as my clients."

In Morley's office, Esme and Molly listened to Morley and Brian and me as we discussed my "plan." After my two colleagues expressed their grave doubts about it, Esme said, "I don't know about all your other stuff—what you saw yourself that time and all the stories you've heard, Uncle Bill—but what I heard and saw down by the lake, and what I saw through the ice and what Craig took a picture of, that's all true. What's wrong with telling the Crown prosecutors the truth?"

After some more unavailing argument, Morley threw up his hands and sighed. "Okay, Bill, if you insist, I'll call Derek Smythe."

CHAPTER twenty-four

Derek Smythe refused to meet with me before he heard from Morley what I planned to say. Morley gave him an outline, and he responded, first with exclamations of utter disbelief at what I was "threatening" to do, and then with an invitation to me to join him and the director of public prosecutions at their offices, with Morley present, for a "clarification" meeting.

In the office of Winston Myers, the director of public prosecutions, I told him and Derek Smythe, off the record and without prejudice, that I was there acting as a parent and a guardian in what I thought was the best interests of the girls, but against the advice of their lawyers. Since I was going to go ahead and do it anyway, however, no matter what anyone advised, everyone with a vested interest in the case should be aware beforehand. They listened to how I proposed to proceed without interruption but with looks on their faces throughout that shouted, "This guy is a raving madman."

Before my last words were out, the director spoke up. "You are an officer of the Supreme Court, Bill, not to mention a highly esteemed civil lawyer, and I gather you are asserting that you are prepared to taint and prejudice a serious murder trial by the public dissemination of rumours, crazed speculations, and preposterous reports of sightings and visions more in the nature of hallucinations and fabrications than reality? I can't imagine better confirmation of the serious drug problem inherent in this case. Now it's not for me to teach you your professional ethics, but I must ask, as one member of the Law Society to another, are you not fearful, not only of being in breach of the law, but also of being censured, perhaps even disbarred and expelled from the Law Society, as result of such reckless, irrational public statements regarding a case before the courts?"

"Thanks for your candour, Winston. Yes, it would appear that I do have a conflict of interest between my duty to the Supreme Court and my duty, as I see it, to children under my protection. Well, I choose to resolve the conflict by attempting to prevent my children from being railroaded into unjust punishment by an overzealous Department of Justice and a government acting politically. And be assured, I shall be saying so publicly, loud and clear. Fear of disbarment—are you nuts? What is disbarment compared to standing by and watching the lives of two teenaged girls being ruined over a stupid adolescent blunder?"

"Okay . . ." Winston Myers paused for effect. "Then what about your disbarment and probable criminal conviction on top of the girls' convictions—three ruined lives for the price of two? Do you like that better?"

"So be it. But no trial, let alone conviction, will happen before full public disclosure of everything I know about the hidden, dangerous monster lurking in Twenty Mile Pond." It even sounded silly to me as I said it.

"The lurking...? Oh, for heaven's sake!" Winston Myers snorted out his derision and shook his head slowly, lips compressed, as he got up.

"And you'd better tell your minister and your deputy minister that, too." Now I was sounding desperate.

"For amusement," said Myers, "I may tell them all about it over a beer at the departmental barbeque next summer, but I can assure you that I will not be interrupting their busy schedules during the workday this winter to relay such irrelevant, peripheral absurdities."

"So they will be hearing my startling disclosures from the media for the first time—about which, I will be saying publicly, I reported to you beforehand."

"Of course, just like every other citizen. Where else would they hear it? You are aware, I assume, that the minister and his deputy are never involved in decisions on police investigations or prosecutions of criminal offences."

Here I was surprised to hear our Morley Sheppard jump in. Though very much against what I proposed to do, he'd had the decency to remain silent until now. "Yes," he barked at the two prosecutors, "uninvolved just like in the Mount Cashel orphanage case, where the deputy minister at the time and the chief of police conspired to thwart the police investigations and prosecutions of Christian Brothers who had criminally abused scores of little boys under their care for years."

"I am shocked to hear you say that, Morley," said Myers. "You of all people are aware of the changes and safeguards that have been effected since those unfortunate times. If you are, however, characterizing the department of today as being at all similar to the way it was in those dark days, please say so directly and unequivocally in order that I may meet the allegation head-on."

Morley smiled, waved his hand dismissively, and said nothing else. Then I said, "As a professional courtesy, I'll wait till I hear back from you before I call my news conference."

The director said, "That's a small professional courtesy, indeed. Bring your press conference on whenever the irrational compulsion comes over you. It's your funeral." He walked over to the door and opened it to signal that our immediate departure from the office was desired.

"Well," I said to Morley, walking down the corridor, "that worked admirably."

"Maybe better than you think, Bill. Their reaction was too extreme for people feeling entirely comfortable."

A couple of days later, Morley called me and said, "I've heard through the grapevine that Winston Myers did report your presentation to the deputy minister and it went on to the minister. Apparently they thought that your intentions were more political than judicial, and that the brass in the department should therefore be made aware.

The speculation is that the premier herself has been brought into the loop on some need-to-know basis."

That buoyed me. Perhaps there would be progress on this yet, but what it might be, I had no idea. Over the next week, nothing happened. If there was in fact some advancement, it was taking an unconscionably long time showing itself. Now I had to decide if I should follow through on my "threat to go public with my outlandish fantasies," as Derek Smythe, the prosecutor, just yesterday had described it to Morley Sheppard, and if so, when.

I let it ride for a few more days, no doubt giving the prosecution the satisfactory impression that they had called my bluff and I had lost my nerve. Perhaps I had. Molly kept asking me, "Dad, but like when?" I started to psych myself up for the promised performance. But before I could act, if, in fact, I was ever going to, Danny Power contrived a criminal undertaking of revenge against the girls.

CHAPTER twenty-five

Morley Sheppard agreed with Derek Smythe that Esme's preliminary inquiry would be held in mid-May. There was nothing to be gained, he told us, by delaying it any longer. April had become so mild a month that the thick ice on the ponds from the deep-freeze winter had thawed, and nearly every evening was pleasant to be out in. Therefore, one fine Friday evening toward the end of the month, Molly and Esme decided they'd have dinner downtown, probably their "last supper," they tried to joke, before the Crown lowered the boom on them.

Craig was finishing his winter semester exams around the same time, and he insisted that they celebrate that rather than engage in the bleak joke the girls had in mind. Besides, he had a friend at the university who, having met Esme at a party that winter, couldn't take his mind off her, he told Molly, and they should ask him to join them, too.

"Todd?" said Esme. "Yeah, sure. He seems to be a nice guy."

Esme had no regular boyfriend. She wanted to get the trial behind her, she told us, to see whether her love life would involve someone studying political science and playing soccer at the university or someone with tattoos in an orange skirt at the women's correctional centre. We tried not to laugh but, as Jennifer said, you always had to laugh at what Esme came out with, in spite of the seriousness of her predicament. And the irony, Esme continued, was that ever since she'd been charged, the invitations to go out on dates were showering down on her like manna from heaven, or locusts, she wasn't sure which.

"Uncle Bill," she said. "You're a man, right? Is there something about a girl being a murderer that turns guys on?"

Before the boys came to our place to pick them up, I cautioned the girls against alcohol. They were still more than a year short of legal drinking age, although they both looked mature enough to get into any club or bar down on George Street, and I assumed they possessed fake IDs. Their release on bail, I reminded them, was conditional on not being involved in any illegal activity whatsoever.

Craig and Esme's date, Todd, were nineteen and legally allowed to drink alcohol, but when they arrived I drew them aside and said that I trusted them not to have anything whatever to drink if they were driving and not to offer the girls any alcohol. The boys assured me on both counts. Then Jennifer and I gave Molly and Esme money to help pay for dinner if they wanted to, and for taxis if necessary.

* * * * *

The police pieced together an account of the fatal events of that evening from various sources—observers, participants, forensic evidence, and Danny Power.

After their dinner, the foursome went to a crowded establishment, the very kind of place that I, the old fogey, had warned them against. There, Craig ran into his former girlfriend, the one he had been going out with just before he and Molly had come together. Craig and the former girlfriend spent a lot of time talking off in a corner alone together. This merely irritated Molly at first, but as it went on, she became coldly resentful in spite of assurances from Esme's date, Todd, that there was absolutely nothing to it. Craig was just tying up some loose ends, he said.

Molly, though, with Esme's encouragement—"You don't have to put up with that crap from him, Molly."—started talking, perhaps in a flirtatious way, with other young men in the place, in order to spite him.

When Craig came back to reclaim his territory, Molly gave him the cold shoulder, and continued to talk and laugh, as if she was having a good time, with a couple of guys hanging around.

Craig said, "Come on, Molly, do whatever you want, but that dude there is a lowlife."

Molly replied, "At least he's not so full of himself he's trying to have two or three girlfriends on the go at the same time."

"There were a few things I had to straighten out with her, that's all. I didn't know she was even going to be here. But it's all done now."

"You took long enough. What were you trying to straighten out—her place or yours after you dropped me off?"

The conversation deteriorated into a tiff and Molly told him she was going to get a taxi home. Craig said, "Whatever," and walked off with an even more pronounced swagger than usual into the crowd.

His devil-may-care body language further exasperated Molly, and she told Esme and Todd she was going home. Esme, rather than have Molly leave and walk over to the taxi stand by herself, told Todd she had to go with her.

Todd didn't like that at all. He said, "I thought you and me were getting along great, Esme. Don't go spoiling our whole night just because those two big babies are gone into a sook."

"Sorry, Todd, I've got to go with her."

"Aw, goddammit. I suppose I'll have to walk you over to the taxis."

"No, you stay here and try to make Don Juan, a.k.a. God's gift to womankind, over there come to his senses."

Outside, Molly and Esme were joined by two young men from the group with whom Molly had been talking and laughing. They were both cold sober. Molly had joked with them that they must be the only other people in the place besides her and Esme drinking Coke and ginger ale. The boys said they never drank and drove.

As the four of them walked toward the taxi stand, one of the guys said, "You don't have to get a taxi. We can drop you off at your house." The girls said thanks, but no thanks.

At the stand, there was a lineup and a fair amount of boisterousness and queue-jumping. One young fellow was being sick up against a wall. The lads with Molly and Esme said, "Come on, we'll drop you off. You don't want to stay here." This time, the girls agreed, and followed them to their car, parked at a distance on a deserted street. "Hard to find anywhere to park down here in the nights," one of them said. "This was the only place we could spot."

When the girls started to get in the back seat together, the two young men didn't even try to press them into splitting up between the front and the back so that they could have the privilege of a man each. The girls looked at each other in surprise. "These guys are too good to be true," Esme murmured.

Then, as they were settling back in their seats, a third man came out of nowhere, pushed Molly brusquely into the middle of the seat, got in, and slammed the door. "Remember me?" he said, leering. "I'm the brother of the guy you killed. And these dudes are his good buddies."

Esme pulled on her door handle. The door didn't open. "Childproof," said the driver, smirking.

Molly looked hard at the man next to her. "You're the guy in the other car at Windsor Lake. You're Danny Power. We're not supposed to have any contact with you."

"When we're finished with you two," said Danny, "contact will be too mild a word for it. Yeah, I'm the dude you're trying to frame for murder."

"What are you talking about?" said Esme. "We never even mentioned you."

"That's not what the cops say. They told me that you two claimed I was down there by the pond and got into a fight with my own brother over the dope money, and grabbed your pole and stabbed him in the eye. I was in the clink for a month before I made bail. Who would you believe, if you were me, a brace of bitches who murdered my brother or the famous Royal Newfoundland Constabulary?" He laughed. "Now there's something to pick from for ya. Listen, whatever. That's not even what I gives a shag about. What I'm doing here is, you killed my brother. I've been biding my time and waiting for my chance and now here it is. B'ys, there is a God. It's payback time. You two are going to get what's due. The boys here will see to that. Hand over your cells."

"I don't know what you guys are planning," said Esme, "but how do you expect to get away with anything? People saw us leave with you two, and the first person the police will suspect is Jason's brother."

"You let us worry about that," said Danny. "First off, the police will have to have some evidence connecting us to whatever goes down with the two of you, and that's not going to happen. Nobody will ever know." He grabbed Molly by the hair and yanked her head back. "You deaf? Hand over your cellphones, I said." The girls complied. He passed them to the fellow in the front passenger seat. "Here," said Danny, "make good use of them. Okay, let me out of here. Like this skank just said, I'm not even supposed to be seen with these two while I'm out on bail."

The driver pressed something and Danny opened his door. Esme tried to open her door, too, but the guy in front was waiting for that and lunged halfway over his seat. He grabbed Esme by the arm of her jacket and pulled her back. Then he seized her throat and forced her hard against the seat, making her gag. "Stay put," he said, "if you don't feel like being strangled right here and now."

Meanwhile, Molly was trying to squeeze out through the other door, but Danny punched her in the solar plexus and she toppled back on the seat, gasping. Her head landed on Esme's lap.

Danny said, "Okay, don't try anything else funny or these dudes will off you without even a heads-up, just like you offed my brother. That's only what you deserve, for sure. But if you keep still, maybe we'll only ruin your lives totally, but at least you might still be breathing. It's fifty-fifty right now. Don't push us. See ya at the safe house, b'ys."

CHAPTER twenty-six

The two thugs drove Molly and Esme across the city, past the Avalon Mall and down Thorburn Road, heading in the direction of Portugal Cove-St. Philip's. They would be travelling by a short section of Windsor Lake.

When the police asked Danny Power later why his buddies chose Thorburn rather than Portugal Cove Road, which was closer to the actual house they were heading for, he replied that none of the boys could stand to go out the Cove road anymore, ever since the Browning bitch murdered Jason on that side of the pond. The police deduced from answers to their questions from other gang members, though, that they routinely took Thorburn Road out because it was less frequently patrolled by police in the nights, and, also, it allowed them to throw off anyone looking for them who might expect them to drive on the more direct road out of St. John's.

This last reason for the gang's driving ploy I found to be true on the night in question after I got a phone call from Craig. He told me he was worried. He and Molly had had a little tiff, he said, and when he went back to apologize to her, Todd told him she and Esme had left to get a taxi. "Let's go find them," Craig had said.

Outside, the girls were not to be seen. Craig and Todd walked over to the taxi rank, and Craig asked a guy he knew there if he'd seen Molly and her friend Esme. The guy responded, "I can't keep up with your girlfriends, man—" He was just being a joker, Craig insisted. "—and there's lots of chicks on the go down here tonight." Craig described Molly and Esme to him and he said, "You mean those two hotties who were just here? I think they were with a couple of Danny Power's buddies. What are they, mules?"

"I don't know for sure if it was them," Craig said, "but it sounds like it. I'm worried. I'm sure they didn't know there was a connection between those guys and Power. Do you think I should call the police?"

"You stay on the line. I'll put you on hold and I'll call the police."

I gave the police the details and told them what we feared had happened, and, within minutes, they'd ascertained from their surveillance records that although Danny Power and most of his associates lived in downtown St. John's, they spent a lot of time in the Portugal Cove area. It was suspected that Jason Power had had the run of a house out there that his gang used as a headquarters, and that the car containing Esme and Molly might be headed out that way.

The police scoured the city roads and Portugal Cove Road, patrolling back and forth, searching, keeping their eyes out for a car described rather vaguely by Craig's informant on George Street. "I think those guys own a blue Ford. I'm not sure—it was dark when I saw it, man."

Meanwhile, Jennifer and I were on tenterhooks, waiting. We called Maggie to see if they were over there, but we didn't tell her anything when she said they weren't. Then we paced the floor, wringing our hands.

At length, police in a patrol car searching for Molly and Esme heard an item on their radio scanner and put two and two together: on the Thorburn Road side of Windsor Lake, a bizarre motor vehicle accident had taken place.

CHAPTER twenty-seven

The police reconstructed what they believed the men in the car had intended for Esme and Molly. The driver of the car had, in fact, been heading for the house, possessed by Jason Power but registered in someone else's name, obscurely located up from the main road in Portugal Cove. Inside this secret house, hidden below floorboards, detectives found cellphones owned by three individual teenaged girls. Saved in each phone were photographs of its young owner in various states of undress and intimate exposure.

The girls in the photos were identified as residents of the St. John's area, and were obviously not professional models. They turned out to be in the lower grades of high school. All three were in police records for suspected drug use and having had their nude images transmitted, together with their names and addresses, in emails, text messages, and tweets, and placed on various social media and porn sites. The photos bore the appearance of being selfies, and the sources of the transmitted pictures and messages and postings were identified as each girl's own smart phone.

One of the girls, whose pictures and information were common on all the social media, was already the subject of an intensive child abuse and child pornography investigation by the police. Her parents had instigated it after she had either attempted suicide or accidently overdosed on cocaine.

The police had discovered from questioning her friends that she had been intimidated into silence about who had done this to her, and that suicide may have been preferable to continuing to live with those gruesome images on the Internet, and the violence done to her and still threatened, and the drug use. She was in hospital, incoherent, but, with luck, recovering from a critical condition, and addiction to crack cocaine.

Another of the teenaged girls pictured pornographically—she was fifteen years old—had been missing for eight months. She had vanished seemingly into thin air and had not been seen since she'd left school on a day early in September before her class was dismissed, having told a friend she was going to walk home, just a half-mile away. There was evidence in her record to suggest she had been close to completely out of control. At first the police had conjectured that she was another runaway, but by now they feared the very worst.

The motives behind the dissemination of the photographs appeared to be punishment and intimidation of the girls for various purposes. One involved a gruesome hint to young drug users to pay up and not buck the gang in any way, or face worse. Another entailed possible forced prostitution, with Internet exposure serving to threaten, demoralize, and discredit these young girls in their own eyes. And then there was enticement, and, likely forced addiction, to narcotics.

It was surmised by the police, based on suggestions from informants, that the missing fifteen-year-old had been forced to prostitute herself to two or three adults at high returns to the gang, and that she had "got disappeared" by them when an implied threat to go to the police made her hazardous merchandise.

The police report on Molly and Esme said the investigators had determined that they had in fact been threatened with the same kind of intimate public exposure and abuse all over the Internet. Danny Power, who broke under police questioning when they told him of the fatalities in the car accident and confronted him with the enormity of the new charges he would be facing—conspiracy to commit murder, child pornography, and sexual assault against minors, for starters—indicated that the driver of the car, his lieutenant, would have used on Esme and Molly his habitual taunt to girls they were brutalizing: "They don't call it the World Wide Web for nothing. And that's where your little oysters and orchids are going—worldwide, duckies." Apparently, the thug's favourite website was the pornographic Oysters and Orchids.

The police concluded that Danny Power and his men intended to punish Esme and Molly through their intimate exposure method, not for purposes of enforcement or intimidation regarding other activities profitable to the gang, but for simple vengeance. What the gang may have intended for them besides the punishment, judging by the missing girl, was too horrific to bear contemplating.

CHAPTER twenty-eight

The initial police report was clear on what actually befell the car that Esme and Molly were in, on Thorburn Road. But how and why it happened was, pending further investigation, still somewhat opaque.

The car had been moving at a moderate speed at first, according to witnesses in other cars, probably at about seventy kilometres an hour. But at a certain point it accelerated to perhaps twice that speed, judging by the distance it flew through the air when it left the road. Certainly, it suddenly began to pass every other car on the road in front of it. The police concluded that the two men had heard on their police radio scanner that police were looking for them on Portugal Cove Road, and so they were racing to arrive at their safe house and hide the car.

Whatever other factors, besides excessive speed, might have caused the driver to lose control of the car, the fact was that it flew off the road and landed in Windsor Lake. But Thorburn Road approached the lake closely enough for that to happen over only a few metres. The window of opportunity was so small that the car ending up in the water had to be an absolute fluke.

After the car was retrieved from the lake and the victims inside removed, fingerprint tests were performed on the interior for any prints that might have remained. Esme's were found overlapping the driver's on the steering wheel. In fact, prints from all four fingers on her right hand were lifted from the top right-hand side of the wheel.

The presence of her prints suggested one theory: although she'd been in the back, she'd managed to grab the wheel and twist it to the right, causing the car to leave the road. Why she would have done that when the car was travelling at such a high speed had not been fully explained at the time of the preliminary report. Another huge question was why two occupants had died and two had survived. It was postulated that it was simply a function of each person's positions in the vehicle, although investigators were not satisfied that that rationale was free of difficulties.

Perhaps the men had been rendered unconscious from the car's sudden impact with the water. Maybe the inflated air bags played a role. In any event, they did not escape from the car, even though their doors were unlocked. They drowned.

The two young women were in the back seat with childproof locked doors. The locking mechanism on both doors was found to be intact after the car was taken from the water, but one back door was swinging on its hinges. Perhaps it had been jolted open by the impact, though the condition of the locking parts was more consistent, according to a locksmith, with the door having been forcibly wrenched open by some powerful force.

The window of that same door was found to be smashed in; hence another police theory was that perhaps one of the girls had been able to open the door from the outside through the broken window. That theory was weakened by statements that the impact with the water had left the girls semi-conscious.

Molly's seat belt was still buckled when the car was retrieved, but one side of it had been torn free of its attachment. How that occurred remained problematic, but it seemed to be what allowed her to float free.

Esme's escape presented less difficulty. She had unbuckled her belt to reach for the steering wheel, and then after she'd turned it, immediately flopped down on the floor of the back. Whatever the details might be, it seemed clear that the smashed window, the open back door, the unbuckled seat belt, and the torn seat belt provided the girls with their seemingly miraculous egress from the vehicle.

Car passengers who had stopped to investigate the phenomenon of headlights shining underwater found Esme and Molly lying side by side on the rocky shore next to the water. The police were not able to locate anyone who had witnessed the car actually leaving the road.

One man driving behind the car in question told police that he was not at all surprised by the accident since the car in the lake had passed him, moving so rapidly that his own car actually shuddered. The female member of a passing couple insisted that she saw the car's headlights moving and jerking underwater. It must have been sliding on a sloping bottom, the woman said, but she could have sworn it was being lifted or pulled. No one else witnessed that.

There were remarks from many observers that the girls must be exceptionally strong swimmers to have been able to make it to shore in that frigid water, which the ice had only recently gone off.

CHAPTER twenty-nine

The police report, compiled from information obtained from their own investigation, a lot of it third-degreed out of Danny Power and remaining gang members eager to save their own skins, and much of it provided by the two girls themselves, was, I knew, somewhat incomplete. There were elements of the story that Esme and Molly had not told the police, but which they did tell me to see if they should do so.

Esme confirmed to me that she could in fact remember unbuckling her seat belt, getting up from her seat, reaching forward between the two front seats, grabbing the top of the wheel, and yanking it to the right, causing the car to leave the road. What she did not, and could not, do right after the incident was explain to the police why she had done it at that precise time and place.

She told me, though, that she could now remember recalling in the car that they would be passing by the lake, and waiting for it to arrive. When she glimpsed the water ahead of the car on the right, she spontaneously acted. She could only say that it felt like exactly the right thing to do at that very moment and that she felt safe and certain in doing it, even though she realized she would be out of her seat belt when the car left the road. She'd been convinced that it was the way, the only way, out of their predicament. It was almost as if, she said, something had come over her, inspired her, to make her act.

Neither Molly nor Esme had any memory of the window being broken or the door opening, but both of them could recall from their dazed and semi-conscious states the sensation of floating to the shore, propelled along almost like a child whirled through the water at a beach or in a pool by the hands of a parent.

They hadn't told the police about how they got to shore, even though they had both experienced the same thing; they agreed that it seemed too surreal to recount. Esme said to me that she had no desire to be treated as a madwoman again, as she had after her description of what had happened beside the lake to Jason Power. Hence, they were not going to inform anyone but me of that phenomenon, at least not until I said so.

A week after their ordeal, when they had recovered from the shock, they related, at my behest, most of their "newly remembered" details to the police, including being carried to shore by some strange force. Then I told Molly and Esme I wanted to announce, right away, my news conference, which would disclose all I knew about whatever mysterious force was in the lake. I thought it might give them a better chance of success at the upcoming preliminary inquiry and their trials. Were they still onside with that?

Yes, they chimed together, they certainly were. I asked them if they were comfortable with my adding all the "surreal" details of their surviving the crash into the lake. "Go for it," they chorused.

I telephoned Winston Myers, the director of public prosecutions, and told him that this was a courtesy call to let him know I was about to reactivate my news conference idea and announce it for this very afternoon. The details of the girls' mind-blowing escape from the car, I said, should be of some interest to all the media, whose newscasts for days had led with stories of the car careening off the road into the lake, the miraculous survival of the two girls, and the deaths of the two punks involved in a vicious narcotics and white slavery ring, and possibly murder, involving teenagers.

The pause at the other end was long enough to prompt me to say, "All right, then, Wince, thanks for listening. Goodbye."

"Wait. Wait a second, Bill. I understand Morley Sheppard doesn't want a postponement of the preliminary inquiry. Which is perplexing, frankly. May I ask why?"

"We want it to go ahead soon after my news conference for maximum benefit to our defence," I said, "and then, if there is to be a trial, we'll be pressing for it to take place at as early a date as possible."

"Bill, please give me an hour to get back to you before you announce your press conference." I told him I would.

Thirty minutes later Padraic Sullivan himself, the minister of justice, telephoned. He was calling me personally, instead of having the director do it, he said, because this matter had public ramifications beyond mere criminal prosecutions. Could I attend an urgent meeting right away with the premier and a small group of top officials who formed a highly confidential loop?

I said I would attend, as long as it was absolutely clear that, by doing so, I would not be surrendering in any way my freedom to act thereafter as I saw fit.

"Understood," he replied. "And as this meeting will not be strictly about legal considerations, may I ask you not to bring the lawyers with you?"

"Well, I certainly won't be able to make any decisions that might affect Esme and Molly in their absence or the absence of the lawyers."

"No, no, of course not," said the minister of justice. "But you'll understand the reason for the privacy and secrecy once the meeting starts."

CHAPTER thirty

At the security desk outside the premier's suite, one of her assistants was waiting for me, and ushered me right into her office. Premier Nancy Russell came around her desk to greet me and shake my hand while her assistant went out to the anteroom to collect the minister of justice, his deputy minister, and the deputy minister of natural resources. They were followed by the Crown prosecutor and the director of public prosecutions.

After some hellos all around, Premier Russell said to me, "Mr. McGill, I trust that your daughter, Molly, and your niece, Esme, are recovering from their nightmarish experience. Please give them my very best wishes."

"Thank you, Premier Russell, they are recovering well. And I note that you have made yourself aware of their names and their relationship to me. The police told me that, as minors when the alleged offences took place, their identities are still being kept confidential and off the public record."

"Yes, I have purposely made myself aware of all aspects of their recent ordeal and, of course, the charges against them. I have received everything, I assure you, on an officially confidential basis. And I have to say that I have never before read a report of a police investigation in which the very same contents both disturbed me to the core—their vicious abduction and probable fate—and relieved me to the core—their extraordinary salvation. Shall we sit, gentlemen? I'll ask the minister of justice to begin."

"Will everyone agree," Minister Sullivan asked, "that everything said here today is completely off the record and totally without prejudice, and that only what is explicitly agreed to by the person stating it can be used for future actions or statements by anyone else?"

We all agreed.

"Now, normally," said the minister, "I, as the political head of this department, do not get involved at all in criminal prosecutions, but take an absolutely hands-off position; all decisions are left to the officials in the division of public prosecutions. We would never allow political considerations to decide whether we prosecute or not. That is why we asked the Crown prosecutor and the director to come here today to give us their frank, off-the-record appraisal, which is theirs alone to make, of their likelihood of a successful prosecution of the charge of second-degree murder against Esme Browning. Gentlemen?"

"Are you suggesting, sir," asked the director, "that we divulge, not only all information, evidence, and names of witnesses, as we have already done under rules of full disclosure to the defence, but that we tip our hand to the uncle of the accused, here, on our strategy and arguments and our assessment of our chances in court?"

"Not unless you're comfortable with it," said Sullivan. "It's your call entirely. I'm sure there's not much that a superior defence lawyer like Morley Sheppard is not already on top of. The only reason we are asking for your frank assessment of a likelihood of conviction is that there is a policy consideration which may be in conflict with a trial. If the likelihood is better than even, or whatever cut-off you use for your decisions on pressing ahead or not, then, of course, go to trial, no matter what the political consequences may be. On the other hand, if the likelihood is low, but you are still proceeding aggressively because of, say, our no-tolerance of illegal drugs policy, then there may be merit in considering whether or not to proceed with the charges. But ultimately, that's entirely up to your public prosecutions division."

Winston Myers gave the impression of musing for a moment. "Well, you're right—we wouldn't be telling you anything here that the defence does not already know or suspect. Let's quickly go through the pros and cons of the case in the interests of transparency. Esme had a strong motive for attacking the victim: an indecent suggestion, touching, a forced embrace, which could be regarded as sexual assault, if jurors were to believe her account. Moreover—"

I jumped in. "Of course, even if she killed the victim, as you allege and which we most strenuously deny, she would still have available to her the defence of self-defence as a result of those same actions by the victim."

"Madam Premier, will I be given the chance to complete my few remarks uninterrupted, or is this to be a free-for-all?"

The premier said, "I see no reason why there shouldn't be a give and take, a back and forth, on each point as it emerges, Mr. Myers. It might give us a better insight into this whole situation as it unfolds in the telling."

"As you wish," said Myers. "Well, a claim of self-defence would be weakened by Esme's assertion that, before the time of death, the victim had removed himself from her and was urinating in the lake—also borne out by the evidence on the state of his trousers: i.e., his fly was open and there were fresh urine stains on the front of them. Sorry, Madam Premier, to have to be so graphic."

"It's quite okay, Mr. Myers, really," said Premier Russell. "Despite my many years of dedicated public service I did manage along the way to pick up on open flies and various human effluents found to have a staining effect on garments. Please proceed."

"Thank you, Premier. The victim's action weakens the urgent necessity of immediate self-defence on Esme's part. And so we are left with the dramatic evidence of the blood on the point of the pole, together with her known skill in its use as a weapon, which well supports the finding that Esme used her hiking pole to pierce his brain through his eye."

"She told you how the blood got on the pole," I said. "She used it to touch and prod the body after he fell and before she knew he was dead. And there's no evidence whatsoever of actual brain material or even eye matter on the pole. As to her dexterity with the pole, it's far from clear at this point that evidence on her use of it in the past to graze a rabid fox will even be admitted by the judge, and I can assure you the defence will be aggressive on that point."

"Well, it must be said here, Madam Premier," said the director of public prosecutions, "that *any* defence or explanation raised by Esme's lawyers would be seriously tainted by the fact that, by her own admission, she and the victim had been involved immediately before his death in a serious criminal offence, the purchase and sale of a large quantity of marijuana. And we are all aware of the public's attitude, and no doubt a jury's attitude, on drug trafficking and serious crimes connected with it, which is basically this: we should throw the book at the perps and then throw away the key. I believe your government's own unyielding policy accurately reflects that attitude."

"But, Winston," I said, "the prosecution would have to contend with Esme's mother giving evidence, sitting there in her wheelchair, paralyzed—I hate to be cynical about this, Premier, but it is a reality the prosecution must face—to the effect that her loving daughter, however misguidedly, was purchasing pot for her for medical reasons, and the defence is prepared to call expert witnesses on its use for that purpose."

"Laying aside all those peripheral matters for a moment," said Myers, "the fact is that the accused does not have a credible defence owing to the obvious fact that the victim had his brain pierced when she was with him, with absolutely no one else there or alleged to be there with them at the time who could have done it. And there was no evidence, forensic or otherwise, that he fell of his own accord, for example, and occasioned the wound from a sharp object on the ground. Nothing along those lines was found."

"No, the forensic evidence shows eye and brain matter containing the victim's DNA to be on and around the broken branch on the tree, which accords with Esme's explanation that he came flying through the air—"

The director interrupted. "The accused's story that the victim came flying through the air and that a broken branch eight feet above the ground caused the fatal injury would appear to be so preposterous in a solemn court of law, however well it might play all dramatized up on television, that I'd be surprised, ultimately, if the defence was to even bring it up before a judge and jury." I saw the premier, and the minister of justice and the deputy ministers, stir in their chairs during Myers's last pronouncement, and exchange furtive glances.

I said, "You can rest assured that it will be brought up, as well as other strong direct and circumstantial evidence supporting the existence of something powerful enough in the lake to do it. And please do not overlook the fact that Esme would be an exceedingly well-spoken and credible witness, plus the fact that the two young ladies do not give any impression of being criminals, let alone murderers or accessories to murder."

"Well, we shall see about that," the director of public prosecutions muttered. "But let me say that, all told and in conclusion, I'd judge that the case for the Crown has a greater than fifty-fifty chance of success. It may not be an overwhelming probability, for some of the more rational reasons given by Mr. McGill, but the circumstances and seriousness of the case demand that it be proceeded with zealously. Is your zero-tolerance war on drugs warranted, one may ask, Madam Premier? Well, the victim had in his possession some dangerous, addictive, life-threatening narcotics, and his brother in the car waiting for him could have passed for a sales agent for a pharmaceutical corporation."

"But is there any evidence," I asked, "that Esme was purchasing hard drugs from him?"

"The police have their suspicions. But no, we do not have a smoking gun, so to speak. And we are well aware that there will be little sympathy for the victim in the eyes of the jurors if evidence of his past criminal conduct, much of it exceedingly unedifying indeed, is slipped before them. He and his known associates and purchasers have criminal records for break and enter, holdups of convenience stores, and serious assault, all in connection with obtaining money to purchase hard drugs, and now there are allegations of physical and mental abuse of girls, no doubt in connection with trafficking to minors and even a possible child prostitution ring.

"Two of those criminal associates, now deceased as a result of the automobile accident, actually used their leader's acquaintance with Esme and Molly, following their purchase of drugs, to abduct them for what appears to be some pretty nefarious and despicable purposes. My point, Premier, is that the word has to get out there to young people that they need to stay as far as humanly possible from such low forms of humanity in order to avoid unforeseen consequences of a far more serious nature than simply toking up."

I was practically shaking with indignation. "Is that also part of this government's zero-tolerance policy—blame the victims for being kidnapped and potentially murdered at the hands of hoodlums who seemed to have been acting with immunity from the criminal justice system? The other victims of the gangsters' abductions and obscene public exposure around the world, are they to blame, too? The missing girl—possibly a dead girl—is she to blame?"

"Mr. McGill. Please," said the director, raising his hand for calm. "No, of course they are not. We do know there was previous connection between the victims and the criminal gang in those other cases, as well. But I will state categorically, to clarify our position against any attempts to confuse the issues, Madam Premier, that there is a world of difference between blaming the victim, on the one hand, and warning young people for their own safety not to associate with criminals, on the other. If I tell my daughter not to walk alone in dark alleys downtown at night, I'm not saying I will blame her if she is victimized, I am saying that for her own safety she should—"

"Quite," said the premier. "So . . . am I correct in my impression, Mr. Myers, that our all-out war on drugs is substantially fuelling your prosecution of Esme for murder, and, were it not for that, there's a fair chance that you would not be proceeding with a charge of murder because of a significant risk of not obtaining a conviction?"

"We would be proceeding," said Myers, "but in the hope of obtaining a guilty plea and conviction on reduced charges— manslaughter, assault causing death, criminal negligence causing death. Anything, really, to hammer home our stated policy of lack of tolerance in drug cases."

"*Now* I understand your policy," I said. "It may not be a case of blame the victim, but of being prepared to victimize two young women as a warning to other young women not to become victims. You have our complete assurance, of course, that neither Esme nor I nor her mother would consent to accepting your bribe to reduce charges, even if our lawyers recommended it, which they most assuredly have not and will not. Esme has told us she wishes that capital punishment were still in effect, because she would rather be hanged than falsely plead guilty to doing something criminal that she didn't do."

I saw the premier suppress a smile. She didn't know Esme, but she seemed to like her style. Then the premier turned to the justice minister. "Do you have any further questions or comments, Minister?"

"Just one further point, madam, and I think it's the crucial one. It's a question to the prosecutor and the director, and it is a genuine question, not a leading question or a hint of any kind on how you should reply—an honest objective question requiring an honest objective answer. If these charges of murder and accessory to murder against the girls were to be withdrawn for lack of compelling evidence or the presence of a compelling defence, would that offend your concept of the rule of law or violate your legal consciences as officers of the Supreme Court?"

The prosecutor and director looked at each other. The minister asked, "Would you like to go back to your office and discuss it? Because it would be entirely your decision based on your best judgment."

The director said, "I think that would be best, sir. We'd want to examine all the angles and be absolutely sure about this, whichever way we decide to go. But I must assert, Minister, that our overriding intention at present would be to press on in the direction we are already heading with the prosecution."

CHAPTER thirty-one

After the premier had thanked the Crown prosecutor, the director of public prosecutions, and the assistant deputy minister of justice and excused them from the meeting, she looked hard at me in silence as they were gathering up their papers and briefcases and leaving. When the office was empty except for the minister of justice, the deputy minister of justice, the deputy minister of natural resources, and me, she said, "I understand, Mr. McGill, that you may be considering going public before the trial with some rather bizarre observations and anecdotes concerning a lake that provides our drinking water."

"There's no 'maybe' about it, Madam Premier. I am going to hold a news conference today and disclose everything I've seen or heard to date on the mysterious happenings in the lake and invite others to contribute what they have seen or learned."

"Are you not a little concerned as a citizen that, with your allegation of some sort of a sinister presence, perhaps even a live monstrosity in the lake, you may cause serious anxiety and alarm? At least three roads run right by the lake within a few feet of the water. And what do you think you would be doing to people's view of the water they are drinking, considered by everyone, currently at least, to be of the highest quality?"

"I'll be brutally frank, madam. I could not care less if it does alarm people. That's small potatoes compared to the possibility of my niece and daughter being railroaded into prison and criminal records and ruined lives in aid of some misguided and overzealous advancement of a government's political position. The more panic the better. If the existence of a monstrosity has already become a factoid in the minds of the public before the trial, then it will make Esme's defence all the more credible in the eyes of the jury. So I certainly intend to go public with it, you can mark that down."

"I already have an idea of the information you possess, but would you mind just touching on everything you know or have heard so that I will be fully apprised?"

"So that you or your colleagues can debunk it all beforehand in the hope of making me look like a kook when I come out with it?"

"Your suspicions are understandable. But I promise you, we will not do that. We'll keep it secret, and I will ask you for a commitment as a lawyer to keep confidential what I intend to tell you. But I believe we do need to compare and share information on this subject."

"On your word that you will not try to use it against me beforehand, Premier, I will tell you." I related my experience with the osprey and the seagull twenty years before, and the stories from residents, including the permanent disappearance of Multi-Million Dollar Man, apparently while he stood alone by the lake, preparing to defile it.

The deputy minister of justice spoke up. "Mr. McGill, that gentleman, also known as Walter Barnes, was the subject of a deathbed confession two or three years ago. One of his old comrades, in a state of dementia at the Hoyles-Escasoni Complex, told some staff members there that he helped kill and bury Barnes. But he died before staff or the police could get any details on the alleged murder or where he was buried, if, in fact, there were any. The police follow-up with others who might have been involved in the disappearance led up a blind alley. But I thought you should be made aware of the confession."

"Thank you, but as you said, a state of dementia and a blind alley." I went on to describe everything else in my grab bag—the governor and his little granddaughter, Tommy Picco's two juvenile giant squids, Professor Atwood's description of the flexibility and adaptability of cephalopods, the snapshot of the "eye," and finally Esme's and Molly's description of what had saved them from certain death.

The premier nodded as I spoke. After I'd finished, she said that although she'd already been told most of what I'd described, hearing it first-hand certainly made it ring eerily true. "The manner of the girls' escape from the car was the clincher for me," she added. "Some might say they could easily have cooked up that salvation story, but I don't think so, not in the light of all the other anecdotal evidence.

To me, this comes down to a choice between either believing Esme and Molly or believing in a divine miracle. As someone who has been in politics for many years, I do not much believe in miracles. Now, what I am about to divulge to you, I must ask you to swear to keep secret just as if you were a high public official. Do you agree to do that?"

I held up my hand as if I was in court. "I so swear."

"The minister of justice, the deputy minister of justice, the deputy minister of natural resources, and I are the only ones who are in possession of all the information I am about to relate. Some of it was given to me by my predecessor as premier in a file marked 'top secret.' There are stories around publicly, of course, but in the nature of tall tales and fantasy. They are easy to dismiss. But your experience and those of your niece and daughter might raise the credibility level very high, especially when combined with your research. That was the main reason the minister of justice and I were hoping the prosecutors might obtain a guilty plea to a lesser charge—so as to avoid a full public trial where everything you knew, or had learned, might come out—yet, at the same time, preserve the good repute of the law. That was before, I assure you, we really accepted your theory, Mr. McGill, of how the drug dealer might have been killed by that branch high on the tree."

The premier paused and looked down at her open file folder. "Now, here's the full situation: reports of sightings of something in the lake have come into the Department of Natural Resources over the years. A few years ago, a maintenance worker in the water treatment plant swore up and down to a fellow worker that he saw a seagull being seized in the air by a snake or an elephant's trunk or the like rising up from the water. Very similar to your own experience.

"Now this man was recorded as having a drinking problem, so it would have been easy to simply dismiss his oral report of his alleged sighting, and forget about it. But his foreman reported it in writing to get the man's drunken hallucination or delirium tremens on the official record. If something went wrong at the plant, his fellow workers wanted management to know beforehand who to blame. The report found its way to the deputy minister of natural resources, because it was so bizarre. The poor worker later died of hypothermia in a snowdrift in the woods next to the lake on his day off, if you can believe it. But that report, combined with some other snippets the deputy heard as a result of his inquiries, piqued his curiosity, and he had the good sense to run a few tests. Please tell us what they indicated, Deputy Minister."

The deputy cleared his throat. "A device for detecting motion and tremors was placed in the lake and it definitely picked up unusual vibrations of an indeterminate nature, but from what source, we had no idea. We had a constant watch kept for a number of weeks, but nothing was ever sighted. One night, we commissioned two wildlife officers, volunteers, whom we'd made familiar with the rumours and the readings, to row a large boat out on the lake under cover of darkness, wearing their night-vision glasses, and confirm to me once and for all that there was nothing untoward going on in the lake. And, indeed, they saw nothing on the surface. Then, with their hearts in their mouths, they told me, they plumbed the depths of the water in various places, hoping against hope that they might disturb something alive down there. But nothing happened except that they discovered something unusual about the bottom.

"What they found in one of the deepest spots was a narrow cave or tunnel. We'll call it a tunnel because they were not able to reach the end of it. The main source of water for the lake is spring water that flows in from the bottom. But this tunnel seems to contain, not an inflow, but an outflow of water, an underwater stream outwards of some force, since it took the sinker right to the end of the several hundred metre line, and still no end was found to the tunnel.

"We don't yet know where the water goes. The altitude of the lake is quite high, about the same as Signal Hill, so there would be a fairly powerful gravity flow if in fact it reaches the sea. We conjecture that if there is anything there in the lake, it could very well hide in that tunnel. Perhaps it travels in and out of the lake to and from somewhere else, perhaps even Conception Bay, though I consider that scenario to be unlikely because of the salt water-fresh water adaptability problem.

"We have thought about sending divers down to explore but decided that, in light of the reports of untoward incidents with other humans, it was unsafe. At some point, if we can do it without being detected, we may send down a small robotic device equipped with weaponry to sedate or even kill whatever might be there, if anything, and bring it up."

"Meanwhile," said the premier, "we want to keep everything as discreet as we can so as not to cause any public disquiet. If you were to go to the media with your story, that could have dire results, we believe, and we earnestly wish to dissuade you from doing it. Minister Sullivan?"

The minister of justice paused before he spoke. "We are prepared to attempt a trade-off with you, not of an ignoble nature that subverts justice, but an honourable one that would keep the lid on this thing, at least for the time being, until further experimentation and exploration can take place. We are hoping that the director of public prosecutions will see fit to drop all charges against Esme and Molly in connection with the death of Jason Power. It's their call, but I have doubts that there's enough direct evidence, and it would be easy for a defence lawyer of Morley's capacity and competence to argue, perhaps successfully, that the death may well have been caused by accident, by misadventure, perhaps a stumble that caused a freak accident.

"It was only today I was telling the premier of a case I recall from a few years ago when I was golfing in Las Vegas. A man charged with assault was found not guilty when his alleged victim was shown to have literally climbed the wall in a frenetic, drugged state, and put out his own eye on a coat hook nearly a foot higher than his height. Not unlike what Esme is alleging. Morley could argue that the hoodlum victim, under some insidious chemical influence, might well have climbed up that tree a couple of feet and jabbed himself in the eye and brain with that branch. Look, who in God's name knows what was going on in his thuggish head? In other words, there could well be enough there to raise a reasonable doubt. So . . . my deputy minister will talk with the director and see what happens."

I couldn't help thinking that the minister of justice had just done a better job of arguing our case against his own department than we were doing ourselves.

There was a limit, though, to his fairness. "It goes without saying, however, that we must proceed with the charges relevant to the purchase of the marijuana. Esme and Molly have admitted to their involvement, and it would look very strange to the police if those charges were dropped. We all remember the Department of Justice's cover-up of the abuse of boys by Christian Brothers at Mount Cashel when Premier Frank Moores and Justice Minister Alex Hickman were in charge, and we can't have anything like that happen again. The police would go nuts. The chief would resign *and* join forces with the police association to condemn us on that one. But Morley and the prosecutor can discuss the extenuating circumstances—Esme was buying it for her mother for medical reasons. Perhaps a conditional discharge for both girls under laws applicable to youth, and the record expunged after three years if they keep their noses clean. That kind of thing."

I told the premier I'd discuss the possibilities with our lawyer and see what they could negotiate with the prosecutors. I'd wait two days for that to run its course before going public.

CHAPTER thirty-two

The negotiations, Morley told us, were by no means a walkover. But he did think that something in the Department of Justice was encouraging a new degree of reasonableness in the Crown. At the end of the first day, Director Myers said to Morley, "The prosecution under our system is not out for blood, or to win at any cost, but is interested in reaching a decision consistent with justice. If, I say *if*, this is a proper case for giving the benefit of the doubt to these young ladies, we would have no problem in principle or conscience in dropping the murder charges." Morley had the impression that the director's heart wasn't really in that statement.

By the middle of the second day, I was getting antsy. I called Morley and he told me that the Crown was still agonizing over the likelihood or not of conviction. They said they were having difficulty reaching a consensus on that. I told him I was going to call the minister of justice to confirm that my timetable was firm:

if there was no deal at the end of today, then my news conference would take place tomorrow morning.

When I called Padraic Sullivan, I was put right through. Even before I could speak, he said, "Bill, I know why you're calling and I say to you: trust the system."

By four-thirty that afternoon, Morley and the prosecutors had reached an agreement. The charges in connection with the murder would be absolutely withdrawn, not just stayed, and all police files and justice files deleted from all and any databases and otherwise destroyed. If a police reference or police background check were ever to be required by Esme or Molly in the future for any purpose, including employment and passport applications, there would be absolutely nothing in existence to report on from those charges. Any official data on Esme and Molly would now be as non-existent as if the murder charges had never been laid.

As to the indictment against Esme for purchasing the marijuana, and against Molly as an accessory, the prosecution would agree that, in return for guilty pleas, and because of the extenuating circumstances relating to Maggie, the Crown would consent to conditional discharges. Their records would be expunged after three years of good behaviour, and at that time, the girls would apply for full pardons. If they had stayed out of trouble in the meantime, their applications would be supported by the Crown.

It was comical and gratifying at the same time, when Morley, Brian, and I told the girls. Looks of relief and appreciation flooded their faces, they gushed out words of thanks, and their embraces of the three of us were prolonged beyond reason. Brian actually blushed when Esme hugged him hard and long, and kissed him on the cheek.

I saw Esme blush, too, when Molly whispered to her, thinking I couldn't hear, "I hope no one snaps our Brian up before you can be actually tried as an adult." Then they laughed, and Esme made a series of little nods at Molly.

Afterwards, when Morley Sheppard and I were alone in his office tying up loose ends, he said to me, "The crusading prosecutors, Derek Smythe and Winston Myers, send you their greetings and their condolences. They said they would like to know, when you can finally get your head around it, what it feels like to be totally bamboozled, and have the wool pulled completely over your eyes, by your own teenaged niece and daughter."

The grin that leapt to my face threatened to split it in two. "Tell them that it was considerably more pleasant than having to listen to two straight shooters spouting truth and justice."

Speaking of the truth, I took Esme and Molly to visit the man whose "old foolishness" helped save them—Uncle Hughie Tucker. It was obvious he had a good idea of what had happened. "I'm pretty well plugged in to just about everything on the go," he told us.

After we thanked him for sharing his invaluable lore with me, which changed the direction of their lives, the girls became fascinated at the hand holding and snuggling going on between Hughie and his fiancée, Maudie. "Oh my God," said Esme to Molly, "I hope that's me in sixty years."

Hughie and Maudie invited us all to their wedding, which was to take place in the chapel at the home in a week. "Now you young ones don't have to come if you're too busy," Hughie said to the girls. "It's only going to be a very informal affair."

Molly and Esme replied, almost in unison, "Mr. Tucker, we wouldn't miss it for the world."

"See, Hughie, what did I tell you?" said Maudie. "Some things are just too nice to miss, even if it's not Westminster Abbey." Hughie put his eighty-eight-year-old arms around her—still strong, judging by the way Maudie's knees buckled and her eyes rolled back and closed in her blissful, seventy-five-year-old face when he squeezed. Molly and Esme looked at each other and smiled wide, their hands clasped over their hearts.

On the way out of the home, the girls walked ahead and Hughie lagged behind, holding me back, wanting to say something to me. "Bill, tell me the truth, did the government lawyers really fall for that malarkey about the monster of Twenty Mile Pond?"

"I can't break a confidence, Hughie. But, yes, something worked."

"Well, I'll be damned," he said, a look of astonished delight on his face. "That crowd is gullible enough to believe anything. And to think that's where my tax dollars are going."

A couple of weeks later, I drove Esme and Molly down to Horse Cove to see Tom and Melissa Squires. I told them that Uncle Tommy and his sister didn't know, of course, that his stories had helped clear them of their crimes, but I did want the girls to meet him as another contributor to their deliverance.

With me I carried a bucket of salt beef I'd bought at Belbin's, and in their house, after introductions, I offered it to Melissa to make some future Jiggs' dinners for them both. She said she'd accept my kind offer if I'd come out for a scoff next Sunday at midday myself, and bring the young ladies and the rest of our family with me. I told her I'd be there, and the girls chimed in that they would, too.

"If my wife, Jennifer, and my son, Matthew, and my sister, Maggie, are able to come, Melissa, that'd be six of us altogether. Wouldn't that be too many?"

"My goodness, no. I've had as many as twenty here. We had to set up two card tables next to the dining-room table."

"That's how famous her Jiggs' dinners are," said Tommy, "and rightly so. My son, they're the best."

"Don't mind him," said Melissa modestly. "I put what he said then in the same category as his old stories about the squids in Windsor Lake."

Uncle Tommy giggled. "What is it you calls me, Liss? A what? A pata-something."

"A pathological liar," said Melissa, with conviction, but grinning. "You and Hughie Tucker up there. The two of you, your whole life. So you'd better be ready for more next Sunday, Bill. I think I'll invite him and Maudie, too, if they're back from their honeymoon in Gander."

"Bring a designated driver with you," said Tommy. "I've been saving that bottle of the good stuff you gave me for this."

CHAPTER thirty-three

Every so often after the murder charges were dropped, and despite the self-confessed unreliability of my sources, Esme and Molly drove to Twenty Mile Pond and looked out quietly over the waves. It was a little pilgrimage, they said, that even their friends were not allowed to join them in performing—nobody could, except me, the one who'd first experienced Twenny so many years before.

I went out with them once, and they said they wished they could sprinkle rose petals on the surface to honour Twenny. But they knew that throwing anything in the drinking water would be misunderstood by observers. "And it might make Twenny mad," laughed Esme. "You know what he gets like."

In their dedication to their hero, the monster, I could foresee a conflict coming up between me and my oath of secrecy to the premier on one side, and my need, in conscience, to tell my daughter and niece everything I'd learned from her on the other. It did, eventually, and I ended up revealing all.

We sat around our kitchen table one Saturday—Jennifer, Molly, Esme, Maggie, Matthew, and I—discussing the monster's future fate. The girls wanted Twenny to be left alone. They didn't want the government or anyone else poking around in the lake, probing any tunnels on the bottom down there, searching for him and trying to capture or kill him. They were prepared to do anything necessary to stop that, and they wanted me to do the same.

"He's harmless if people just stay away from the lake," said Molly, "like they're supposed to, anyway."

"There's no evidence he has ever intended to hurt anyone," said Esme. "He didn't mean to kill that Jason Power guy. That was a freak accident. He only meant to move him away from the pond and stop him from polluting the water. I'm afraid poor little Twenny just doesn't realize his own strength."

"All the evidence is that he either saves people," said Molly, "like the governor's daughter, and me and Esme, or he leaves them to their own devices like the governor and his man or those thugs in the car. It's not his fault if people like Danny Power's guys die from their own evil."

"What about Multi-Million Dollar Man?" I asked. "A death sentence for using the bathroom in the wrong place?"

"There's not a shred of evidence, as Mr. Sheppard would say, that Twenny had anything to do with his disappearance," said Molly. "If he is dead, he was killed by his own gang, and he's pushing up daisies in a shallow grave overlooking Conception Bay.

Or, if he was alive when he left, I'm with Mr. Tucker on that: Multi is down in Columbia or somewhere, running a drug cartel. So we shouldn't use guys like him to make Twenny look like a homicidal psychopath."

"Right," said Esme, "and Twenny didn't even touch those two kayakers a couple of weeks ago."

She was referring to a story that had been on all the newscasts. I'd been startled when I'd heard it. Two kayak enthusiasts were visiting from Ontario and decided, in their unfamiliarity with the place, to launch their craft in Twenty Mile Pond and paddle about. After an hour or so, when they finally understood the signals from the police on the shore meant that they should get off the pond, they came in absolutely unscathed.

"I can only conclude," I said, "that those two mustn't have thrown any waste into the water. Twenny didn't even tip over their kayak."

"He's very intelligent and aware," said Esme. "He knows exactly what's going on. I'm sure he was sorry he got me in all that trouble. His eye through the ice was very sad, just as sad as the bull moose's. I think Twenny was happy he could make up for it, when the car went in the pond."

"You say 'he,'" I said, "but it sounds to me like it's a she, or, if it's a he, he's definitely on the girls' team, the way he only saves girls and either bumps off the guys or reluctantly lets them survive on their own."

"I'd rather believe that those two guys in the car got exactly what they deserved, and it had nothing to do with their gender," said Esme. "It would have been the same if it had been women."

"Who's going to blame Twenny for not saving the likes of them?" asked Maggie. "The only thing that went wrong in the whole thing was that that thug Danny Power wasn't in the car, too. But he'll be inside for a good while with all those extra charges against him, especially the child pornography and sexual assault charges. And when he does come out, it'll probably be in a shoebox. Don't other inmates in prison kill guys like him who abuse children? They used to, in the good old days. I hope they still do."

We were all surprised by Maggie's vehemence. But no one took issue with it. We went quiet for a while. Then Maggie said, "By the way, I'm not always going to be as crotchety as that. My doctors have okayed me as a candidate for medical marijuana. They think it might work. And even if it doesn't, at least it'll mellow me out."

Everybody laughed and cheered, and Esme said, "See, I told you. And they all thought I was just a juvenile delinquent." We laughed again, but a little more nervously this time at the way Esme may have put her finger on a bit of a tendency in her makeup.

Jennifer broke that ensuing silence with a change of subject. "Talking about Twenny's attitude to men, Bill, what about you? She certainly saved you. And from a fate worse than death, the way you told it, when the sight of the seahawk and the gull and the tentacle made you turn around and come back from your suicide mission."

"Yes, Dad, she brought you and Mom together. So please keep in mind that you owe Twenny big time, too."

CHAPTER thirty-four

I'd been thinking, leading up to this conversation around the kitchen table, about whether or not I should release publicly all the information and stories I possessed about the monster of Twenty Mile Pond.

But what about my oath of secrecy to the premier? Well, I'd concluded, she only made me do it to shut me up for her own purposes. I was grateful she did intervene to get the girls off the hook, but before I threatened to go public, everyone on the government side had been prepared to railroad Esme and Molly into jail to score some political brownie points. And for what? Because the "murder" of a vicious thug had been associated with the sale of drugs? Marijuana, for God's sake, which was in the process of being decriminalized just about everywhere in the civilized world. Therefore, I figured, I was never truly bonded to my promise. I was coerced into making it and, figuratively, that was the same as if I'd crossed my fingers behind my back.

Satisfied that, morally, I could disclose all I knew, my next question to myself had been, should I? Well, it might save people's lives if they were aware of the peril of doing something stupid in or near the lake. But more important, it might help save Twenny. The mere possibility of her existence might make her such an icon to people everywhere, and a magnet to fascinated persons wishing to survey the surface of the lake in hopes of catching a glimpse, that the government would be obliged to leave her alone. Because, otherwise, the outcry would be too great.

I raised all this now with my family in the kitchen and asked them to discuss with me whether, for those reasons or any others, I should share with the world our stories of the existence of Twenny of Twenty Mile Pond.

I was met with a chorus of yeses.

"Let's make him or her," said Matthew, "a national treasure." He gave Molly and Esme another hug, an action he was prone to perform half a dozen times a day since the night they'd escaped alive from the car in the lake.

"If you do, Uncle Bill," said Esme, "and I really mean this—I promise to be good from now on."

"Esme," I said, placing an arm around her shoulders and squeezing, "I can't turn that offer down."

Maggie seemed to concur. "Yay-y-y Twenny," she cheered, and then giggled at length, a behaviour so out of character since her accident that I could see everyone wondering if her doctors might not have already given her a sample of that new medicine she'd been prescribed.

It made Molly, Esme, Jennifer, Matthew, and me rise from our chairs and gather in a ring around Maggie and touch her, and smile and laugh at each other through our tears.

"The world will know," I said.

ACKNOWLEDGEMENTS

My heartfelt gratitude to Susan Rendell for editing this book. It was a great pleasure to work with her again and receive her creative insights. My sincere thanks once more to graphic designer Graham Blair for his superb cover. And, as always, my wholehearted appreciation to Garry, Jerry, and Margo Cranford, and to Laura Cameron, Bob Woodworth, Peter Hanes, Randy Drover, and Gerard Murphy, all of Flanker Press, for their dedication to publishing, marketing, and distributing the book.

Born in Newfoundland, Bill Rowe graduated in English from Memorial University and attended Oxford University as a Rhodes Scholar, obtaining an Honours MA in law.

Elected five times to the House of Assembly, Rowe served as a minister in the Government of Newfoundland and Labrador, and as leader of the Official Opposition. He practised law in St. John's for many years, and has been a long-time public affairs commentator, appearing regularly on national and local television, as well as hosting a daily radio call-in show on VOCM and writing weekly newspaper columns.

Rowe has written eight books: *Clapp's Rock*, a bestselling novel published by McClelland and Stewart and serialized on CBC national radio; *The Temptation of Victor Galanti*, a second novel published by McClelland and Stewart; a volume of essays on politics and public affairs published by Jesperson Press of St. John's; the critically acclaimed political memoir *Danny Williams: The War with Ottawa*, which appeared on the *Globe and Mail's* bestsellers list in 2010; *Danny Williams, Please Come Back*, a collection of newspaper articles covering social, political, and economic issues; *Rosie O'Dell*, a critically acclaimed crime novel published by Pennywell Books, a literary imprint of Flanker Press; and *The Premiers Joey and Frank*, which was a *Globe and Mail* bestseller in 2013, and which the *Hill Times* selected as one of the Best 100 Books in Politics, Public Policy, and History in 2013.

Rowe is a member of the Writers' Union of Canada and has served on the executive of the Writers' Alliance of Newfoundland and Labrador. He is married to Penelope Ayre Rowe CM of St. John's. They have a son, Dorian, a daughter, Toby, and three grandchildren.

Bestselling author Bill Rowe dishes up a long-awaited tell-all memoir that covers the years he spent in the political arena with Newfoundland premiers Joey Smallwood and Frank Moores. *The Premiers Joey and Frank* is three stories in one. First is Premier Joseph Roberts Smallwood's, whose ego and force of personality dominated every room he walked into, and strained to the breaking point every personal relationship he had. The latter half of the book covers Premier Frank Moores and his mixed personal motives, combined with a singularity of political purpose: Get Smallwood. Entwined in both these stories is that of Bill Rowe's own roller-coaster political life, where family and partisan politics were often inseparable. This is a riveting, entertaining, and often hilarious account of three men who aimed high, Icarus-like, and who earned three very different places in the history of this province.

#8 on the *Globe and Mail* (Canadian Non-Fiction) Bestseller List
(October 12, 2013)

#8 on the *Globe and Mail* (Biography) Bestseller List
(October 12, 2013)

Selected for the *Hill Times*'s
Best 100 Books in Politics, Public Policy, and History in 2013

Rosie O'Dell is a creature of beauty, brilliance . . . and unspeakable secrets. When she was young, terrible crimes had been committed against her. Tom Sharpe became Rosie O'Dell's high school sweetheart, and in revenge for the transgressions against her, the two young lovers committed their own crime of passion together, which ultimately ripped them apart. Thirty years have now passed since Tom has seen his Rosie O'Dell, and the intervening years have been a source of endless torment for him. He has been torn between yearning for his lost love and wanting never to see her again. These days, Tom is a successful lawyer in the city of St. John's, but trouble seems to have a way of finding him. And now here she is: Rosie O'Dell has returned to ask for his help once more. Tom Sharpe will soon find out that his troubles are just beginning. Critically acclaimed author Bill Rowe's political memoir, *Danny Williams: The War With Ottawa*, was a *Globe and Mail* Bestseller. The novel *Rosie O'Dell* marks his long-awaited return to the realm of Canadian fiction, where fans will agree he is a master at the game.

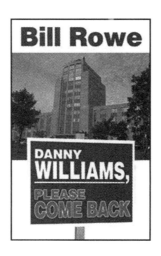

Bill Rowe, author of the critically acclaimed political drama *Danny Williams: The War with Ottawa* (*Globe and Mail* Bestseller, 2010), is back in fighting form and ready to throw a few more punches at the local, national, and world leaders who fill our lives with endless amusement and exasperation. Rowe's newspaper columns, written between 2005 and 2007 and collected here for the first time under one cover, are a tour de force that challenge the reader to take on political lightweights and heavyweights alike, societal ills at home and abroad, and always question motives and demand answers from those in power. Peppered with the same dry wit and humour that propelled this author onto a national stage, this collection is, quite simply, a must-read.

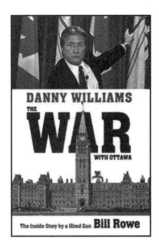

In 2004, Danny Williams, premier of Newfoundland and Labrador, hired veteran politico and popular radio talk-show host Bill Rowe to represent his province's interests in Ottawa. This memoir covers the eight months Rowe served with Premier Williams during what became widely known as the Atlantic Accord Crisis and a bitter, long-lasting feud between Williams and the top brass on Parliament Hill. Combining high drama and hard-hitting analysis of the ruthless game of federal politics with hilarious commentary on the very human side of those involved, *Danny Williams: The War With Ottawa* is the story of a defining time for Williams and his political career . . . and the story of a premier every Canadian came to love or hate.

#2 on the *Globe and Mail* (Canadian Non-Fiction) Bestseller List
(October 16, 2010)

#4 on the *Globe and Mail* (Non-fiction) Bestseller List
(October 16, 2010)

#25 on the *Hill Times* Top 100 Books Published in 2010
(November 22, 2010)

#11 on the *Hill Times* Editors' 15 Picks (November 22, 2010)

#23 on the *Globe and Mail* Top 25 (Non-Fiction) Bestsellers of 2010

#4 on the *Quill and Quire* (Trade Paper Non-Fiction) Bestseller List
(January/February 2011)

#14 on the *Quill and Quire* (Canadian Top 20) Bestseller List
(January/February 2011)

Visit Flanker Press at:

www.flankerpress.com

https://www.facebook.com/flankerpress

https://twitter.com/FlankerPress

http://www.youtube.com/user/FlankerPress